# Sharing Strength

Renee Jean

Text Copyright 2021 Renee Jean

No part of this book may be reproduced in any form or by any electronic or mechanical means, including information storage and retrieval systems, without express permission in writing from the author. The only exception is by a reviewer who may quote short excerpts in a review.
This is a work of fiction. Names, characters, places and incidents either are products of the author's imagination or are used fictitiously. Any resemblance to actual events or locales or persons, living or dead, is entirely coincidental.

This book is dedicated to all those who fought to survive the trauma of PTSD, both those still fighting and those who lost their battle. No one is alone, we are all struggling together and we can overcome.

# Chapter 1

The Clydesburg VFW Hall sat at the end of Memorial Drive on the south side of town. Surrounded by mature trees and a well manicured lawn, the building appeared bright and welcoming from the parking lot. On the inside, however, it was dark and dated. Dr. James Kurtsman stood surveying the long room that was the entirety of the Hall basement. The main floor, accessed from the road instead of the parking lot in the back like the basement, was full of offices and the small reception area. The walkout basement was the home of a number of events and meeting groups like the one he was preparing to host.

Hands on hips, he scanned the dingy digs. The light coming through the grimy egress windows was less than stellar and the doors that opened onto the back lot allowed enough light to enter the building but died in the shadows within a few feet. The flourescents cast a dull glow in pools along the room but there was no complete illumination. Finally he settled on the far end of the room as the best spot. He made his way down the corridor, setting his boxes of donuts and cookies on the counter of the tiny kitchenette then set about making coffee. He was early but a jolt of caffeine would help him be ready. He still wasn't completely sure he was the best person for this.

As he filled the filter with coffee grounds and started the urn, listening to the brew percolating, he mentally ran through the things he had been told about the possible attendees. Because of confidentiality he didn't know specifics but he was aware each of the people coming, or hopefully coming today, had suffered some type of trauma giving them a diagnosis of post traumatic stress disorder, or PTSD.

Before he retired Dr. Kurtsman had been a trauma therapist but he had been out of the game for over five years. Life had been a rollercoaster since his time with patients and technically these weren't his clients, they were Dr. June's, he was just there to give them another outlet. Their healing paths were entirely up to them. He would be a listening ear and do what he could but his stomach still turned over at the idea of leading anyone again. He had never had any problems in previous groups but this one was a little closer to home.

He had been told it would be a small group, even if everyone showed up, and Dr. June was almost positive at least one wouldn't come. Dr. Kurtsman wasn't surprised about the expectation of a lack of turnout for the fledgeling support group. Clydesburg wasn't a big city after all. It was part of the heartland, farms and a close knit community that took care of its own for the most part. It wasn't completely rural but it would never be in the same category as Chicago or St. Louis.

He smiled to himself, remembering the first day he had opened his office downtown over forty years ago. He poured himself a cup of coffee and added some milk. He snatched a cookie from the box and set out a chair from the rack leaning against the wall. He sat down and began flipping through articles on the news sites on his phone while he waited. Replace the phone with a newspaper and it was practically a mirror for that first day in practice all those years before. He had been even more nervous with his first client, hoping he remembered everything he had learned in college and wishing he had decided to do anything else with his life.

That first day went much more smoothly than he expected. He only had a handful of people come to him and most had been people with simple issues who mostly just needed a listening ear and to hear their feelings were valid. The last person to enter his office that day had been Vivian, a young woman looking for a job and inquiring about his need for secretarial work. He had told her he barely had clients so there wasn't really anything for her to do but she insisted on them discussing the prospects of employment over a light supper. He had been so charmed by her he not only hired her but two years later he married her as well.

The memory brought a smile to his face and an ache to his heart. His eyes drifted toward the ceiling. *Give me strength Viv, I need you right now.* He turned his attention back to his scrolling. As he scanned an article about a new medical breakthrough he heard tentative footsteps coming toward him. He didn't look up but saw the beat up running shoes and old jeans going by. He heard the coffee urn dispensing then one of the boxes being opened and closed again. A moment later a man who appeared to be in his mid-thirties placed a chair near him and sat to eat his donut. Dr. Kurtsman lifted his eyes to the newcomer who saluted him with the remaining half of his pastry before pulling out his own phone.

While the man was engrossed in his device Dr. Kurtsman examined him closer. He believed his first guess at age was correct but at least part of that time had been hard lived. There were dark bags under the man's bloodshot eyes and his cheeks had a few days worth of stubble. It wasn't the trendy look he saw on models and actors but more that of someone who simply didn't have the energy to shave for awhile. His clothes were clean but old. There were holes and worn marks around the cuffs and edges and his shaggy hair had been left to do as it wished atop his head.

The man looked up, noticing the inspection. "Can I help you?"

"Sorry," Dr. Kurtsman slid over closer and held out his hand.
"Dr. James Kurtsman, you can call me James if you like. You're the first to arrive."

"Do I win a prize?" He asked in a flat voice, eyeing Dr. Kurtsman's hand. When he didn't shake or offer his own name, Dr. Kurtsman moved back where he had been and resumed his scrolling on his phone. He checked the time and noticed the meeting was supposed to start in ten minutes. As he was looking down he saw movement out of the corner of his eye. Again, he didn't look up but sat back, holding the phone higher to give a better peripheral view.

There was a young girl, very young, pressed into the corner. She appeared to be watching the men. He was about to address her when voices rose up outside. Both Dr. Kurtsman and the other man turned toward the sound. He couldn't be sure but Dr. Kurtsman believed there was an argument headed their way. With the doors closed the conversation is muffled but there were two distinct voices. A minute later the door was thrown open and the owners walked in.

"See dude, there isn't even anyone here." One of them said, his silhouette crossing its arms across the chest.

"This is the place and time I was told. Are you sure there isn't anyone?" The other seemed to lean forward as though trying to reach through the darkness.

"Are you questioning me again? You think because you have a higher rank you always know better? It was a stupid idea to come anyway, there is nothing wrong with you and there sure as hell isn't anything wrong with me." The first man spun around, about to push open the door again when Dr. Kurtsman spoke up.

"If you're here for the support group we are down here." He called through the gloom.

"See, I told you there was a meeting." The second one prodded, making his way toward Dr. Kurtsman's voice. There was a disgusted sigh from the first voice but nothing further for the moment. When they reach the final pool of light the quieter one grabs a couple chairs and begins setting them up near the other two men. He works efficiently. His eyes were downcast, focused on his task. The other sauntered to the kitchen counter pouring himself a cup of coffee and snatching up three cookies. He came back over, dropping heavily into the chair farther from the other men and eyed them.

The man who had been setting up the chairs slumped his shoulders further as he saw his friend's handful of treats and understood none of it was for him. He trudged to the counter to retrieve his own refreshments. He carefully added milk and sugar to a cup of coffee then selected a single donut. Once he had what he needed he took the open chair between his friend and Dr. Kurtsman. He picked at his donut, sipping from the steaming cup. He was still staring at the floor as he waited for things to start.

After wolfing down his second cookie and taking a large bite of the third, the disruptive one looked at the man to Dr. Kurtsman's left. He leaned forward, elbows on his thighs and looked the man up and down. "Hey man, what're you in for?"

The older man gave him a weary glance then returned his gaze to the door at the far end of the hall. The one sitting next to him gave him a slight punch in the shoulder. "Brian, leave him alone, will you?"

"This is stupid. What the hell are we supposed to do anyway?" He leaned back again, crossing his arms across his chest as he shoved the last of his cookie in his mouth. Talking around it he asked, "Isn't therapy just touchy, feely crap for whiny women. Something for people like her?"

All of the men turned to look at the girl who had edged her way around to the counter and was trying to get some coffee while also appearing to do her best to remain invisible. When Brian pointed her out she froze. Her deer in the headlights expression exposing her terror. When no one spoke she finished getting her drink and walked stiffly over to the chairs, setting one up far away from the men. Brian looked like he was about to comment but the other man jumped in first. "Are you ok? Would you like to join us?"

She shook her head emphatically, shrinking further into the shadows at the edge of their circle. Brian muttered something no one else understood and the older man shot him a hard glance again.

"Relax man, this is just "therapy", it isn't like any of this is life or death, jeez."

At that, the older man got up and stalked back out through the front doors. Dr. Kurtsman watched him go as the two younger men began arguing again. "God Brian, what is your problem? Why do you always have to harass everyone?"

Brian's jaw clenched. "You might outrank me at work Kyle, but let's remember I have been the one in charge our whole lives. I'm not harassing him and if he is going to be so sensitive maybe this girly little whine fest is the right place for him but you know darn well there is nothing wrong with me."

They started in on each other again. Dr. Kurtsman watched them for a moment, leery of leaving the scared young girl alone with them but he wanted to check on the other man. After another few moments of internal debate he got to his feet and made his way outside. He found the man sitting on the retaining wall of a garden, smoking. He was watching the parking lot and didn't look over when Dr. Kurtsman joined him. Parked on the far side of the lot was a burgundy car. In the driver's seat was a girl maybe a few years older than the one inside. She was talking, he thought to himself, and was clearly in turmoil. Dr. Kurtsman thought there was a good chance there was a similar debate happening in the car as there was going on inside the hall.

She looked up finally, seeing the men watching her, and her face turned the color of her car. She reached over to her passenger seat, doing something they couldn't see, then emerged with her purse and something in her hands. She squared her shoulders and kept her chin level with the ground. The look of defiant strength was very convincing but it didn't reflect in her eyes. She walked past them and into the dark interior as Dr. Kurtsman and the smoking man turned to watch her. As soon as she was through the doors they could see her shoulders slump slightly and her hands were holding the cuffs of her hoodie sleeves.

She disappeared into the gloom and Dr. Kurtsman checked his watch. He looked up to find the other man watching him. "What do you say we get this thing started?"

The other man's gaze drifted back to the door where the young woman had just gone. He then glanced out at the nearly empty parking lot before returning to face Dr Kurtsman. "Is this all of us? There has to be what, like four of us?"

"Five actually, six if you count me." From the expression Dr. Kurtsman could tell he wasn't considered part of the group officially.
"If anyone else straggles in late we can catch them up but Clydesburg is a small town; I'm sure this will be a fine start."

The other man shrugged, smashed out the remaining bit of his cigarette then followed Dr. Kurtsman back into the building. They were immediately confronted with what seemed to be the endless voices of the two younger men still heatedly debating the merits of the group. They reached the end of the hall and saw that the new girl had set up a chair directly across from the fighting duo and the younger girl was now sitting right next to her. They weren't talking but simply sitting close, observing the argument.

Dr. Kurtsman clapped loudly, bringing silence to the room and all eyes looked up as he made his way back to his seat. "Good morning everyone. My name is James Kurtsman, I am a retired psychologist and used to work with Dr. June. I believe you all have been seeing him and while I wasn't given specifics because of doctor / patient confidentiality, I do know that you are all dealing with PTSD or Post

Traumatic Stress Disorder."

"Or everyone is a big crybaby and y'all are too weak to just deal with life and so you want to come here and whine for no reason." The complainer blurted out. He smirked as he looked around until Dr. Kurtsman jumped to his feet.

"People are here because they want and need help. If you don't want to be here, you're welcome to leave. If you stay you will respect this group, what it stands for, and those that are here to share." He walked over to stand right in front of him, thundering, "Is that understood?"

He received a snort in response but no argument. He looked around at everyone else asking if they were, indeed, in the right place. They nodded carefully, glancing sideways at one another. Satisfied, Dr. Kurtsman made his way back to his chair.

"Why don't we go around and introduce ourselves? Give your name and anything you feel comfortable sharing." He looked directly at the loudmouth still sulking across from him. "Since you like to talk so much, how about we start with you?"

The young man sat up, straightening as much as he could and gave his defiant smirk again. "Fine, I'm Specialist Brian Nickerson of the US Army. My bro Kyle here, dragged me to meet you all even though there is nothing wrong with me. I just came to show him we're fine so we can get back to doing what we do best, kicking ass for America."

He started pumping his fist in the air chanting USA, USA. No one joined in. He glared at everyone, especially Kyle, before crossing his arms and returning to his sulking. Dr. Kurtsman looked next at Kyle, giving him a gesture to go ahead. He took a deep breath, leaning his elbows on his knees and tried to look around at the group. After a moment he faltered and his gaze returned to the floor. His voice was much quieter when he spoke than Brian's had been. "My name is Kyle Masters. I'm a staff sergeant in the Army with my friend Brian. We grew up together as brothers and now serve that way too. We were recently deployed with our squad and the deployment ended with a gunfight not all of us survived. I'm here to hopefully learn new ways to deal with the stress I have felt ever since."

Brian snorts and punches his friend in the arm. The dismissal of his feelings makes Kyle's face fall. He returns to staring at the ground. A look of sympathy briefly floats across Brian's features but when he looks up to see everyone staring at him he darkens once more leaning back in his chair.

Dr. Kurtsman gestures for the third man to go. "I'm Craig Stillwell. Currently unemployed and just trying to get things in my life back under control."

"Anything else?" Dr. Kurtsman inquired.

"Dr. June, the one you mention before, he was treating me after I was in a car accident." He clasped his hands tightly. "I was ordered to go through anger management and then stayed with it after I was diagnosed with the PTSD thing you said. I am still trying to understand it all."

"So you got into a fender bender and what, punched a guy? Or maybe got punched for causing it? What were you doing, texting while driving? Stupid reason to go crying and whining about your problems." Brian laughed.

With no warning at all Craig was up and out of his seat, standing so fast the chair fell over. He grabbed Brian by his collar, yanking the younger man within inches of his face. "That accident ended my marriage and killed my four year old son you asshole. I don't care how tough you think you are or how little you think this is worth, some of us need it. Do you understand me?" He roared the last part while shoving Brian so violently back into his chair he nearly toppled over.

Brian had no response. He sat perfectly still, staring up at Craig who was still standing over him. Once he was satisfied Brian wasn't going to say anything further Craig returned to his place, righted his chair, and sat back down. He was breathing hard and his hands were balled into fists but when he looked over and saw the girls cowering and huddled together his entire body sagged. He looked away, wiping tears before they could fall. Brian watched closely, his eyes shifting between Craig, the girls, and Dr. Kurtsman.

After a few tense moments of silence Kyle looks up at the girls. "What about you two?"

The older girl, still watching all of the men closely while holding the cuffs of her sleeves and massaging her right wrist with her left thumb, sat up slightly and cleared her throat. "My name is Jasmine."

"Nice to meet you Jasmine." Dr. Kurtsman said. "What brings you to us today?"

"Um, I guess it was because I was in a relationship that ended badly." Before anyone can say anything she rushes on, glaring at Brian. "It was mostly my fault. I mean, my parents don't think so but they weren't there, you know? Anyway it ended and now I am trying to deal with that and maybe understand how I can be better in the future."

Dr. Kurtsman gave a pained expression. He had seen people blame themselves many times and usually they were among the most innocent of all but were manipulated into believing everything that could or had gone wrong was somehow on them. It was a mentality that was difficult to break and he made a mental note to talk to Dr. June about his suspicions. He wanted to question her further but seeing her shrink further inside her sweatshirt and whatever the wrist rubbing thing was about, he could see now was not the time.

With an effort he pulled his gaze away from Jasmine and turned to the younger girl who remained slightly outside the circle. Her chair had slid behind Jasmine's when the girls cuddled together during Craig's outburst. He motioned her forward, which she obeyed, reluctantly. When she had reentered the circle he smiled. "Would you like to introduce yourself?"

"Rachel." She blurted. "My name is Rachel Morris."

After that there was silence. Everyone waited but she said nothing further. As all eyes remained fixed on her Dr. Kurtsman could see her begin to panic. Her breathing increased and her eyes grew wide. She was on the verge of an anxiety attack. He got up to help her but she instantly jumped back behind Jasmine, hiding away from him. He holds his hands up in surrender and gently backs away from the shivering girl. He had seen many survivors of abuse. Her reaction to him now and the careful watch she kept over the men in the group led him to be sure he knew what type of abuse she had sustained. The fear shone brightly in her eyes as she got her breathing back under control. His heart broke for her. He was sure she was the one Dr. June had been concerned about. She might not be ready for a group like this.

Brian leaned forward, asking callously. "God, what the hell happened to you princess? Did daddy beat you up or something?"

Before Dr. Kurtsman had a chance to reprimand him again Rachel looked him directly in the eye and shook her head violently. She wrung her hands then looked around the circle. "Three months ago, I was raped."

The room fell into complete silence. No one knew how to respond to her. Finally Dr. Kurtsman asked if she wanted to say anything more. With tears brimming in her eyes she asked if she had to but he told her no. With that she once again gave a quick but definite shake of her head before inching ever so slightly back toward Jasmine.

Dr. Kurtsman looked around the tiny group. Everyone had a name and a story. Some they knew a little about, others were still obviously guarded. That thought made his eyes jump back to Jasmine and by proxy, Rachel. The girls were clearly more reserved than the men although Brian may be the toughest of the all to bring into the fold. Each would take their time and he was prepared to put in the effort as long as he could to help them.

"Is there anything specific anyone would like to discuss today?" Everyone looked at the rest of the circle but no one said anything.
"Ok then, next week we can begin sharing and delving deeper into what brought you all here, any triggers you may be feeling or coping mechanisms you may be using or wish to explore. If there are no further questions I will see you all next week."

"Aren't we all supposed to hold hands and pray or something?" Brian asked surprising the group.

"I believe you are thinking of Alcoholics Anonymous. They usually end with the Serenity Prayer but I guess we can include that if it's something you all would like to do."

Rachel shot to her feet. "No praying."

Jasmine, though the look on her face was as startled as the rest, supported Rachel's declaration. "Yeah, I'm not big on having to pray. We can go to church if we need religion."

Rachel, eyes still brimming with unshed tears, shot Jasmine a grateful look. Dr. Kurtsman nodded, got to his feet, and began putting away the snacks. When everything was packed away he put his chair back on the rack, slid the two the girls had been using and put them away as well, then picked up the boxes of treats and made his way out of the building. Brian watched him leave, then got up, put his own chair away and punched Kyle's shoulder. Kyle didn't say anything but followed his friend's lead and when he was done they left, back to their quarreling.

Craig stood and stretched then looked over at the girls who were still standing uncertainly together. "Was there anything you needed? Anything I can do?"

Rachel hugged herself and shook her head while Jasmine pulled at her sleeves, her left hand starting to rub her right wrist again. They walked out together, awkwardly silent. When they reached the entrance they saw Dr. Kurtsman was standing near the door. He waved and walked over, looking directly at Rachel. "Would you two mind if I had a moment with Rachel?"

Instantly Rachel pressed herself against Jasmine, using the older girl to shield her. Craig stepped back, turning toward the parking lot and making his way slowly to his car. He lit another cigarette as he went, looking back over his shoulder a few times as he walked.

Jasmine eyes the therapist carefully. She reached back with a protective arm, guarding Rachel and the younger girl laced her fingers through Jasmine's. The look of surprise was brief but Dr. Kurtsman saw it. He watched her stiffen for just a second then take a strong step in front of Rachel. "Anything you want to say to her you can say in front of me as well."

He sighed. "I am concerned that this may all be too much for you right now Rachel. You're trauma was quite recent and people can lash out in therapy groups. It may be better for you to continue with individual therapy with Dr. June and try again later. Or if you need a group of people to speak with maybe ones you are closer with such as friends and family would be a good idea. I just don't want to see things move to quickly for you and have you unable to heal the way you so obviously want to, does that make sense?"

Rachel stepped around Jasmine, however she never let go of her hand. She looked Dr. Kurtsman directly in the eye. "I am not a patient of Dr. June. My only conversation with his office was to find out about this group." She took a deep breath, blinking away tears.

"I appreciate you trying to protect me but sadly I can't talk to anyone else. I have nowhere else to go."

# Chapter 2

As soon as the car door closed Brian slammed his fist into Kyle's shoulder. "Dude, what the hell did you drag me to that whiny little pity party for, huh?"

Kyle sighed as he glanced sideways at his best friend. He put the car in drive, pulling away from the VFW hall and heading toward Brian's place out near the edge of town. The whole day was going to go like this, he could feel it already. Once Brian got on a tangent about something the situation would be brought up again and again until he had beaten the subject to death, revived it and killed it again. There was no way to stop it even though Kyle knew he didn't have the energy or patience to get into the subject right now.

He had found the meeting interesting. He knew many soldiers dealt with PTSD and other issues after serving. He had heard first responders like police and paramedics could also have symptoms from what they saw day to day, although he wasn't sure it compared to being in a war zone. But what about the girls? Or that Craig guy? Was it possible they had similar trouble after situations that had nothing to do with military service? He had never considered that before.

"I would like to remind you that you agreed to go. You could have said you didn't want to but you went by choice and then spent the entire time just pissing people off. I think Craig was about to punch you in the face." Kyle kept his eyes on the road as he spoke.

Brian snorted from the passenger seat. "That old man? Please, I would drop him like a bad habit. Not that I have any bad habits myself." He laughed. "I'm as solid as they come. You've seen me in action. I'm cool as a cucumber."

"Oh yeah, nothing gets to you." Kyle rolled his eyes. "Solid as a rock, that's you all the way."

Not noticing the sarcasm dripping from Kyle's words, Brian continued. "Exactly, see you get it. There is no reason to hang out with those crybabies. We have better things to do, like get my damn car running. It is still acting up and I want to take a road trip in it at least once before we head back from leave."

"We will work on the car. I promised I would help and I will, but I have things I need to get done as well."

"Like what? You got some girl I don't know about?" Brian laughed.

"I am going to the services in Arlington for the guys from the squad. I promised Riviera I would go with him. You're going aren't you?"

Silence greeted this. Kyle looked at Brian out of the corner of his eye. His friend was staring, unblinking, out the windshield. His features had darkened like a storm cloud at the mention of their fallen friends. The tension in the car was so thick Kyle felt like he was choking on it as he waited for Brian to say something, anything. Finally Brian broke the silence. "Of course I'm going. A soldier does his duty."

Kyle wanted to point out that it wasn't actually an order or duty to attend the memorial services but the tone of Brian's voice told him such a comment wouldn't be welcome. Anytime the subject of their deployment or the soldiers awaiting burial came up Brian's mood would change dramatically. The whole point of going to the group was to deal with what happened but how could anyone help if he shut down and wouldn't discuss it or how it made him feel? Kyle shook his head, steering the car through the quiet streets. Brian was just a younger version of the man his father had been. Life long soldier but also a trouble maker. Neither liked or obeyed authority well even though they swore to uphold the chain of command.

Brian's refusal to follow the rules and need to prove he should be in charge in Afghanistan had been one of the biggest triggers of the fire fight. The image of his men lying in the road, blood mixing with dirt as the sun glared down on the scorched land flashed through Kyle's mind. The sound of automatic gunfire that sounded like it would never end rang in his ears. Brian was saying something but Kyle couldn't hear him. He was half a world away.

A sharp pain in his shoulder brought him back a minute later. The present came screaming back into focus. They were in Brian's neighborhood but a few houses past his. Kyle blinked away the remaining images, turning to look at his best friend. Brian was studying him closely. "What the hell man? You drove right by my house."

Kyle could tell he was pissed but Brian was always mad about something it seemed. "Sorry, guess I got distracted."

"You guess? I don't think you heard a word I said. Why do I even talk to you? It isn't like you care about what is really important anymore. You haven't been right since we took off. I thought getting stateside you would calm down but you are just not functioning optimally soldier. Get your shit together."

Kyle turned around, drove to Brian's place and parked in the driveway. There was a little electric car parked in the road in front of the house. Kyle looked over at Brian. "Is Dylan here? That looks like his car."

Brian made a sound of disgust deep in his throat but didn't respond right away. Dylan was Brian's younger brother. Daniel Nickerson had been a soldier through and through and while Brian had walked in his footsteps exactly, Dylan had turned his back on the military way of life. He was a pacifist, a poet, and dedicated his life to being a peaceful activist. He was about as far from his brother and father as one could get. Because of that Brian and Daniel had essentially disowned Dylan when the boys were growing up. Kyle had become almost a replacement.

As a foster kid Kyle never felt like he belonged anywhere. When he met Brian they weren't even teenagers but there was no question of the family dynamic for the Nickersons. Brian and Kyle played soldiers in the park at the end of the street almost everyday and learned about the ways of the Army from Daniel while Dylan read, studied on his own, and worked on art projects. Kyle was the only one who spent much time with the younger Nickerson making him into a sort of liaison within the family. Daniel didn't neglect his son with food, shelter, or any of the things people normally associate with survival. He wasn't cruel to him in any way. He just had no interest in the things Dylan was passionate about and when he was forced to attend an art exposition or some other event that wasn't military related he would, at most, be going through the motions.

Dylan wasn't bitter and never showed any resentment toward his dad or Brian. He was mature beyond his years and seemed to understand his simply didn't fit in with the rest of the family. When he was accepted to college on scholarship it was Kyle he told, not his blood family. He kept in touch with Kyle while he and Brian had been overseas and he was the one who had informed them when Daniel had passed away right as they finished basic training. He also chose to step aside and let Brian and Kyle make all of the arrangements fitting for a soldier. Dylan stood by, paid for his share of the funeral, and attended as the spectator he had been most of his life.

"He has some things in storage here. He called and said he wanted to pick up some of his old books. I was hoping he would be gone by now." As they walked toward the front door Dylan came out carrying a box. He looked at Brian, giving his brother a small nod. When he saw Kyle his face broke into a wide smile. He set down his box and embraced Kyle, who was more like family than Brian had ever been.

"Hey Kyle, how have you been?" His tone is friendly but his searching eyes show genuine concern.

"I'm doing ok." Kyle responds as he lets go of Dylan. "How have you been?"

"Things are moving along. Working on finishing my masters while debating what I want to pursue when I'm done. Things were on hold for a bit when dad died but thankfully you guys were here to help with that." Brian snorted, checking his watch and throwing Kyle a look. Dylan glanced over his shoulder at his brother then stooped to pick up his box. "Thank you for giving dad the memorial he would have wanted and deserved. I wouldn't have had any chance of figuring out the military aspects of the funeral. Sorry we haven't talked much since then."

"You had to go back to school and after boot camp we went off to training then got deployed. You just focus on your schooling. You're doing great." Kyle clapped Dylan on the shoulder then turned back to Brian. "Ok man, I see you are ready to get to work. Lead the way."

Brian wasted no time heading toward the house. When Kyle walked through the front door he was transported straight back to his childhood. The house was filled with military memorabilia top to bottom. Flags hung on nearly every wall, soldier statues were lined up in cabinets, and the only books visible outside of Dylan's old room were war stories and biographies of long dead generals. Kyle remembered the first time he laid eyes on this house at the age of ten.

   He had moved in with his most recent foster family but was already feeling the fact he was nothing more than a check to them. He struck out to explore the neighborhood when a boy in army fatigues approached him, asking if he wanted to learn the ways of a soldier. Kyle had nothing else planned so he shrugged and followed the other boy home. The house looked like every other one on the block from the outside but the inside was a completely different world. It looked like a combination of a strategic planning office and a military bunker. Daniel, Brian and Dylan's father, was out in the garage working on rebuilding the engine of a classic hot rod. Brian explained completing the build was the mission of the week and if Kyle wanted to join them he was welcome but had to earn his keep.

   Kyle knew nothing about vehicles and said as much but Daniel said he would teach him and Brian told him a true soldier does whatever it takes to complete the mission. Dylan was home, writing poetry in his room while Kyle learned his first lesson about being a soldier and following orders. Over the next several weeks Kyle did, in fact, learn a lot about how to fix and refurbish a car. He got to know Brian and Daniel very well. It wasn't until the fourth week they hung out that he learned about Dylan's existence when he came out to the garage to remind his father about the art exhibition he was taking part in that weekend.

   Daniel nodded without enthusiasm. When Kyle asked Brian who the kid was he told him it was just his stupid brother with a wave of dismissal. Neither Daniel nor Brian seemed interested in talking about him any further but Kyle was curious about Dylan so he excused himself to get a drink and went in search of the younger boy. Dylan was surprised to see Kyle looking for him but proudly showed off his art pieces and the latest poem he had been working on.

Kyle was shocked at how different the brothers were but when Dylan told him he wasn't much a part of the family because he didn't care about the military Kyle just nodded in understanding. Brian and his father were obsessed. Even after just a month that was clear. Daniel had been a mechanic in the Army until he got injured. His back gave him terrible trouble and after awhile his superior officers had decided a medical discharge was the right course of action. Daniel may not be serving anymore but his mind and spirit never left. He raised his sons with the same precision and order he had been under while a soldier and Brian absorbed it body and soul. Dylan humored his father but made it clear he would follow his own path of passivity.

After that first meeting Kyle would do his best to spend a little time with Dylan during each visit if possible. He felt for the kid that seemed isolated within his own family. As a foster kid bounced around from home to home, Kyle could relate to not fitting in. They were close although Kyle kept that a secret as much as possible out of fear he would be cast out from the surrogate family he found with Brian and Daniel. It wasn't perfect but it was a family who cared about him.

When Daniel died Brian inherited the house. Dylan still had things in his old room but he slowly seemed to be removing them. The rest of the house was exactly the way Daniel had left it. The entire house was a shrine to the Army and Daniel's expectations of the way life would go for his true son. Brian always told stories about his father's time serving and speculated if he had stayed healthy he would have been a general. Kyle was sure that was untrue considering how Daniel had struggled with authority. It always struck him as strange that someone so dedicated to serving and the military order of things would reject the notion they had to follow orders.

Brian was the spitting image of his father right down to the temperament. Just like Daniel, Brian believed he should be in charge of everything, all the time. He was reprimanded for not following orders or the chain of command and had, in the worst example of his ego to date, initiated a firefight that killed almost their entire squad. That situation had been right before they returned stateside. When they got home Brian pushed for Kyle to move in with him at his dad's place but Kyle said he needed his own space to get used to being home.

He found an apartment downtown Clydesburg that rented by the month and moved his few possessions in that same day. From the first night in the apartment Kyle had suffered nightmares and flashbacks. He woke up drenched in sweat, screaming into his pillow. Three days of that was enough and he had called Dr. June with the number his Colonel had given him when preparing to return home. Kyle talked non-stop at the first meeting about everything he had seen, dreamt about, continued to deal with, Brian's reaction to him and the issues, and his debate about returning to service when his leave ended.

Dr. June asked if Kyle would like to bring Brian in for one of the sessions to which Kyle's only response was bitter laughter. He told Dr. June there was no chance Brian would come to a therapist's office. That was when the suggestion of the support group came up. It took over a week for Kyle to wear down his friend and get him to agree to go. In the end though, Brian did agree, stating Kyle would just have to pay for the beer after they got done wasting their time.

"Yo, you gonna help he with my car or what?" Brian called as he flipped the cap off his beer bottle and headed for the garage. Kyle took another look around then snatched a bottle for himself and followed behind his friend.

# Chapter 3

Dr. James Kurtsman shuffled into the VFW hall with the boxes of pastries balanced in his hands. He knew he brought too much considering the size of the group but he wanted to make sure there was enough variety for everyone to find something they liked. He made it to the end of the hall without dropping anything and as he placed things on the counter he thought about the balancing acts the others seemed to be dealing with at the moment.

Dr. June had been over for dinner the previous night and while he revealed nothing specific he mentioned some of his concerns about the members of the support group. He was shocked to hear Brian came to the meeting after what Kyle had said in their sessions. The news he was combative and borderline abusive followed with what Dr. June would have expected. He did mention he had never met Brian, he was just a part of Kyle's group as far as he knew. He also acknowledged to never speaking with Rachel. When Dr. Kurtsman explained her extreme aversion to men and admitted she had been raped Dr. June said he could only imagine how she was handling things at such a young age. He asked about her outside support group but Dr. Kurtsman said he wasn't able to get much out of her.

Jasmine came up and Dr. June was interested to hear what she shared. James looked at his friend. He told him she shared her name and that was all. She was a closed book. Craig on the other hand seemed ready to share. He was hurting deeply over the death of his son and blamed himself. Dr. Kurtsman was sure it was a strong case of survivor's guilt possibly compounded by his wife, or ex wife depending on where they were in the process. Dr. June had sipped his bourbon and nodded with his former colleague's assessment. They spent most of the rest of the night discussing how best to help the group and how Dr. Kurtsman was dealing with being pulled out of retirement to work with them. Dr. June said he wished he could be a part of the process but he was sure his involvement could make things awkward as they chose what private pain to share and what not to. He didn't want his presence to make anyone feel uncomfortable of obligated to share anything specific they weren't ready to tell. They both agreed it was better to keep the separation and Dr. June could continue to treat them one on one if needed.

Now, as the coffee began to percolate, he hoped he was the right person to lead this group. Dr. June's assertion that keeping them different from the private sessions was right on the money but that didn't mean Dr. Kurtsman was the first choice. Considering his own issues he was worried he wouldn't be the best example for the group.

With everything laid out and ready he took his seat facing the door at the far end of the hall. He pulled the book he was reading out of his bag and found his spot. Within a minute he appeared lost in the story. He chewed slowly as he turned the page while down the hall, Craig walked in.

After a moment his eyes adjusted to the dim light. He made his way down toward the doctor without saying a word. He picked up a chair from the stack along the wall, setting it up next to Dr. Kurtsman. He lowers himself into his seat slowly, back rigid, hands gripping his knees as his eyes fix on the door. Out of the corner of his eye, Dr. Kurtsman watches him. The tension radiating from his stiff muscles told a story all its own. He was clearly waiting for the soldiers, most likely Brian, preparing for the battle to come. After last week, Dr. Kurtsman couldn't say he blamed the man one bit. He would have to keep a close eye on the situation to make sure it didn't get out of hand.

After sitting statue still for almost a full minute, Craig got up, walking over to the refreshments. Dr. Kurtsman never lowered his book but he was still able to observe Craig sneaking a flask from the inside pocket of the light jacket he wore. The smell of whiskey floated across short space as Craig flavored his coffee. Once he had a cookie and a donut on a plate he took his place next to Dr. Kurtsman again. As he took a long drink from his cup he seemed to relax slightly though his eyes never left the door.

The sound of a car door closing out in the parking lot made both men sit up a little straighter. The apprehension of Brian and Kyle arriving, if it was indeed them, made both men's hearts race. They waited, side by side, barely breathing but nothing happened. No one came bursting in through the door and no loud voices cut through the air. Craig looked a question at the group leader who shrugged in response. They waited another minute but when there was still nobody in sight Dr. Kurtsman set his book aside, stretched, and walked down to see if he could recognize the vehicle they heard. As he closed in on the door the glare from the sun fades and he can see the third car in a spot on the far side of the parking lot. It looked like the one he had seen Jasmine in last week but he didn't see her.

He pushed through the door and stopped short when he spotted Jasmine crouched in front of the flower bed next to the door. She held a small camera up to her eye, adjusting the lens. She was completely engrossed in her picture and didn't see him standing there. She appeared to be zooming in to get pictures of bees as they danced among the flowers. He watched her just as closely as she studied the garden.

"What are you doing?" The sound of Rachel's voice made Jasmine jump up with a yelp. Even Dr. Kurtsman had missed her arrival. The sudden movement made Jasmine drop her camera and when she reached for it a bee landed on her hand and stung her.

"Ouch! Damn that hurt." She sucked on the finger already turning red. She looked over at Rachel who looked like she might cry. "Are you ok?"

"I'm sorry. I was just curious what you were doing. I wasn't trying to hurt you." Tears are threatening to fall as she looks at Jasmine.

"I'm so sorry. I'm such a complete failure."

Jasmine looks at the younger girl, not sure how to respond. Finally she walks over and puts an arm around her in a side hug. "Bees are jerks. Besides I'll have the last laugh, now that he stung me, he died. We're all good. I got stung a lot as a kid but no biggie since I'm not allergic. Relax, you didn't do anything wrong."

Rachel gives her an uncertain look but tries to smile anyway. "So what were you doing?"

"I was taking pictures of the flowers and the bees that pollinate them. I was looking for small signs of beauty, that's all." She looks embarrassed as she waves dismissively with the camera. "Sounds silly I know."

"You really think there is beauty here? Or anywhere?" Rachel looked around with her watery eyes. Jasmine didn't respond right away. She, like Dr. Kurtsman, was studying Rachel more closely. The girl was wearing baggy clothes, her unwashed hair hung limp against her face which looked gaunt even though she was shoving chips in her mouth from a family sized bag every few seconds. It was like she was actively trying to look as undesirable as possible. It was a natural reaction after going through a sexual assault like she had but the contrast from the previous meeting where she had been plain but well kept was dramatic.

Finally Jasmine slides the camera into her purse and looks over her shoulder at Dr. Kurtsman. The eye contact startles him. He wasn't aware she knew he was standing there. Not knowing what to say, he opens the door and gestures for them to go ahead of him. Jasmine holds a hand out for Rachel. "You ready for the meeting?"

Rachel shrugs, looking at Dr. Kurtsman for the first time. Her eyes flit to the open door then back to his face. Jasmine squeezes her hand reassuringly but she still doesn't move. With a sigh Jasmine lets go and starts toward the entrance. "You don't have to come but I think it is helpful so I am heading in, come if you want. As Jasmine disappears inside Rachel pulls her oversized sweatshirt tighter and runs to catch up. Both girls stop inside the door while their eyes adjust to the change in lighting. Dr. Kurtsman, who was already inside, adjusts quicker and walks down to his chair while the girls move more cautiously.

   When they reach the end of the hall Rachel makes a beeline for the cookies while Jasmine sets up chairs for them opposite from Craig. She looks up to see Rachel has a handful of treats along with her chips. She shakes her head but says nothing as she gets a cup of coffee and takes a small chocolate frosted donut. Rachel sits in the farther chair and stares around.

   Dr. Kurtsman wasn't surprised by the chair Rachel chose and he sees Jasmine doesn't seem upset or shocked by it either. In fact, when she takes her own seat and has a clear view of the door as well as both the men currently in the room he decides she probably planned it this way. Before the girls have a chance to settle in and relax there is one more slamming of car doors from the parking lot. At first no voices follow but after a moment the already familiar sound of men arguing can be heard as Brian and Kyle storm into the hall. The sound of Brian's voice cuts through the silence and every time he speaks both Jasmine and Craig seem to tense slightly.

   The silhouettes of the men move through the doorway where one stops but the other proceeds. Without waiting for his eyes to adjust to the darker space, Brian stumbles over a piece of chipped tile and falls to a knee. Kyle comes forward but the second he gets a hand around Brian's arm his friend pulls away again, obviously even more pissed than when he walked in. Kyle opens his mouth to say something but Brian glares daggers at him before turning away and stomping down to the gathered observers.

"What the hell are you all looking at?" He snaps. The challenge in his eyes stops anyone from commenting but Dr. Kurtsman notices that at the outburst Jasmine slid her chair closer to Rachel who seemed to have shrunk further into her sweatshirt. Brian gets a cup of coffee while Kyle quietly sets up a chair for himself and one for Brian next to him. When Brian turns around and sees the chairs together his eyes narrow. He walks over, snatches the empty chair, and slams it down on the opposite side of the circle from Kyle. He then returns to the refreshment counter to get a handful of cookies.

"You could leave some for others man." Kyle says without getting up.

"Oh, I'm so sorry, are we still waiting for the tour bus to stop by?" Brian replies through gritted teeth. "Get off my back. You do nothing, can't follow through on your promises, and now you want to get upset because I am eating the cookies? That is what they are there for this exact reason. Why don't you just shut up and try a donut of cookie yourself. Maybe some sugar will help you."

"Why do you always have to start drama, Nickerson?" Kyle rested his elbows on his thighs as he leaned forward, staring down the man across from him. "Why can't you ever accept that things don't operate just on your schedule and there need to be allowances made sometimes?"

"Don't start with me Kyle. You know damn well why I am pissed and I have every right to be so let's just get this show on the road so we can actually get something productive done with our lives later." He rolled his hand in the air with a "let's get going" gesture and devoured half of his current cookie with one bite. Kyle hung his head, got to his feet and went to get his own cup of coffee, shooting an apologetic look around the circle as he went.

When he returns to the circle Dr. Kurtsman gets up. "Well, it certainly seems like we have some things on our minds this week. I want to touch on everything, make sure everyone has the chance to share what is happening with them right now, but first I want to look further into why you are all here to begin with. Does anyone know what PTSD is, as in what it stands for and how it can affect a person?"

Rachel starts to raise her hand but when she looks around and sees she is the only one she quickly puts it back down, hugging herself tightly. Jasmine reaches over and squeezes her hand, making her eyes widen and she looks over at the older girl with appreciation.

"Don't be scared Rachel." Dr. Kurtsman encourages. "What did Dr. June tell you about it during your sessions? If, of course, you are willing to share that with us."

"Um, nothing."

Dr. Kurtsman frowns. "What do you mean nothing? What did he say when you saw him? Did he, in fact diagnose you with PTSD?"

"I never went to any sessions. My parents don't believe me about the rape. They blame me. I haven't been able to talk to them about it and if I tried to get help for anything they would just ignore me or yell at me again. I am on my own."

Her robotic answer stuns the small gathering. She seems to grow smaller under their scrutiny. Dr. Kurtsman stares at her. Finally he gets his composure back and asks her, "If you never went to see Dr. June, how did you know about the group or the diagnosis?"

"After I stopped going to school I would spend my days at the coffee house near my house, The PJ Cafe. No one bothered me there and since my parents don't care what happens to me now they never asked where I was going." With a trembling hand she wipes away tears. "One day while I was in there on my computer a girl came in with someone and I overheard them talking at a nearby table about PTSD and a support group through Dr. June. I knew my parents wouldn't pay for therapy but when she said sounded interesting so I looked it up online and called the office to get more information."

Jasmine had by that point moved right next to Rachel. She put her arm around the girl's shoulders and pulled her into a side hug. Even though Rachel's tears continued to fall there was a tiny smile on Jasmine's face. Dr. Kurtsman was about to ask her about it when Brian's voice broke in. "What are you so happy about princess?"

Jasmine's smile disappeared instantly as she turned an icy stare on him. "If you must know, you prick, I remember that conversation. I went to the PJ Cafe with my mom a few months ago and we were talking about this group. I remember telling her I was hopeful it would be a resource for people who really needed the support and help. She is here and clearly she doesn't feel like she has much help other than here so I am happy she heard me talking about it."

Rachel looked up into Jasmine's face with shock and amazement. Brian leans back in his chair, arms folded across his chest, and stares at the girls. Dr. Kurtsman looks from Jasmine to Brian and back again before clearing his throat to reagin the center of attention.

"There is no wrong way to come to us Rachel. You are welcome here. I am sure your parents care but may be struggling with how to help you. We can certainly address that if you would like."

"There's no point but thank you." Rachel says, again in that robotic tone while shaking her head.

"Ok, well for anyone who doesn't know, PTSD stands for Post Traumatic Stress Disorder. It can also be referred to as PTSS substituting Syndrome for Disorder. Either way you prefer it means the same thing. You went through a traumatic event or situation and are now dealing with the after effects. There is a common misconception that it is something that can simply be gotten over or because that particular event may not have caused the same reaction in another that those struggling are faking it. While it is a form of anxiety, it is so much more than that."

"Or people are a bunch of attention seeking crybabies." Brian mumbles. Dr Kurtsman turns to him but Rachel explodes out of her chair, jumping so close to him he backs up a few inches.

"Nobody cares what you think!" She screams, her voice breaking with emotion. "Just shut the hell up. If you don't want to be here, fine, there's the door." She waves her arm toward the end of the hall. "But the rest of us want to be here and you need to stop being such an asshole."

Everyone felt their jaws drop at her outburst. Now it was Dr. Kurtsman's turn to attempt to suppress a smile. Who knew she had it in her? Brian opened his mouth like he wanted to say something back but the way she looked at him made him close it again. Satisfied, she turned and sat down again. As soon as she looked around and noticed everyone looking at her she pulled her knees to her chest and hugged her legs. Dr. Kurtsman wouldn't have believed it possible to curl up in a ball on one of the hall's folding chairs but she was managing quite well.

With everyone quiet again, Dr. Kurtsman looked around at each of their faces. "Many people think just like Brian here. They want to dismiss PTSD and tell those suffering to "grow up", "stop crying about nothing", "get over it". The air quotes seemed to stab at each person as he kept eye contact with one person after another. "I have heard those phrases and so many more as long as I have been treating patients. What most don't understand is that it is an anxiety disorder but the trauma is so intense that it can actually change the chemical makeup of your brain. The effects are long-lasting, usually for years if not permanent on some level."

Craig sat straight up at that. "Well then what the hell is the point of being here?"

"Amen brother," Brian held up a hand for a high five. Craig ignored him, looking at Dr. Kurtsman instead.

"The triggers can last a lifetime and the trauma will always be a part of you but it is possible to heal to the point those triggers don't feel like they are controlling you and to find coping mechanisms that are healthy and helpful. You are here to find a way forward and a support system for when those issues come up out of nowhere."

"Sitting here talking about the accident isn't going to stop my divorce from finalizing, it isn't going to bring my son back to me. And now you are telling me there is a good chance I am going to have the flashbacks of that night for the rest of my life. Why don't I just go put a bullet in my brain?"

"Those are the exact feelings we are here to deal with. Your memories will always be with you but there will come a day when you see a picture of your son and don't instantly remember the accident. Someday you will remember happy times with your wife and it won't carry an aftertaste of bitterness. Eventually the nightmares fade, the flashbacks get fewer, and the memories won't feel like they own you. When you're first starting out on the journey it can seem impossible. You feel alone and like no one will ever understand you. That's not the case though, even though you all came to be here along different paths, you have so much more in common than you know."

Dr. Kurtsman watches his words sink in. He doubted anyone expected to be cured there, except maybe Brian, but he can see hearing how hard the work could be still shook them. He waited, sure the realization would prompt at least one exit from the group. To his complete surprise though, not even Brian got up.

"What brought you to therapy, or here directly? What is your pain point? What is it that's haunting you?" He raised his hands to calm the fears he saw jumping into everyone's eyes. "The questions are rhetorical. My point is that as scary as it seems to face them now, down the road you will find you can not only talk about it but may even be able to do so with others going through something similar. The first part of the journey is finding a way to understand that, while traumatic, what you went through wasn't your fault. When you stop blaming yourself, you can begin the phase of healing."

"What about if it actually is my fault though? I was the one driving. I'm the reason my son is gone. How am I supposed to accept it isn't my fault when it actually is?" He didn't wait for a response. The tears came hard and he doubled over, body shaking as he sobbed. Before Dr. Kurtsman could make a move, Kyle shifted his chair closer and put a hand on Craig's quaking shoulder. Without looking up, Craig reached up and placed one of his own hands over Kyle's. They sat like that for a full minute before Craig spoke again.

"Would it be ok if I shared my story?"

Dr. Kurtsman sat down, gesturing that Craig had the floor. When he didn't start right away Kyle leaned over toward him. "Take your time. We are all here for you."

Craig wiped away a few last errant tears and gave him a tenuous smile. "I don't know where to start."

"Just tell us what you remember, man." Kyle told him. "Start before the accident and tell us how you ended up there."

"I got a promotion." Craig barked out a laugh. "It was completely unexpected and I called my wife to tell her about it. I wanted to go to dinner to celebrate but she said it was too late to find a sitter. We thought it would be ok to bring Jeremy along. He was so well behaved. When we got to dinner she started in about what she thought we should do with the extra money I would get from the raise that came with the promotion. I disagreed with spending it and wanted to save most of it for Jeremy and for the future. She got upset and started drinking more. She had a habit of getting argumentative when she drank so I wanted to get home. The fight continued in the car though and we were still going at it when the car veered off the road."

"Dude, you were in the middle of an argument. It sounds like she might have started it and was the one to keep pushing things. You were trying to avoid a scene. You didn't do anything wrong unless the tree was the way you were trying to end the fight." The entire group turns wide eyes to Brian as his words seem to come as an attempt to comfort Craig.

"I'm sure you did the best you could." Rachel said from behind her still closely held legs.

Jasmine turned back to him. "Craig, what happened next?"

"I was trying to keep things civil and under control. You're right about that but it wasn't enough. She took him out to the car but was so mad at me she didn't check his seatbelt. I was in such a hurry to get home I didn't check either. I let him down." There was a loud sniffle and Dr. Kurtsman got up to grab some napkins. Craig accepted them with a tight smile. "After we left the road I couldn't make out where we were going. The car bounced and was thrown around. I felt like I was on the worst carnival ride of my life. We finally stopped when the front of my car slammed into a tree."

All the color drained from Rachel's face at that. She looked at Craig with haunted eyes. "You hit a tree? That sounds so terrible. You're lucky to be alive yourself Craig."

"I blacked out during impact. I don't remember the airbags going off or anything else. When I woke up there were lights flashing all around me. I asked several times where my wife and son were but everyone was so focused on getting us out of the wreck and to the hospital no one told me anything. There was one man I sort of remember. He checked on me and stayed with me until I was taken away in the ambulance. I don't know his name but I think he may have saved my life." Everyone in the small circle is hanging on his words. "I passed out in the ambulance again and things are fuzzy from when I got to the hospital until Patricia came in and told me I killed our son. The hate in her eyes is something I will never be able to unsee and something I will always deserve."

"Craig," Dr Kurtsman began, trying to keep his voice as steady as possible. "No one deserves to feel hated in a time like that. She was emotional and that is completely understandable but you were hurting as well. Everyone deals with grief in their own way but just because she placed the blame on your shoulders doesn't mean it actually belongs there. It's hard to see, especially if you've been blaming yourself all this time, but you really aren't at fault. Things are rarely that black and white. It is perfectly fine to be upset. You most certainly have that right, as your wife had the right to be upset and even to lash out and blame you. Your hands were the ones on the wheel that night but I have no doubt there was a combination of things that led to the accident."

Craig's tears continued to flow as he looked around the group. He finally looked up and Dr. Kurtsman, the pain etched in ever line of his face. "So I am just supposed to sit here and say it isn't my fault? I am supposed to agree and get over it? Don't you think I have been trying to move on? My sister was with me after the accident and she did everything she could think of to help but here I am in the same place emotionally and hurting more than ever. I'm broken. There is no saving me and I don't deserve it after what I stole from the world."

Dr. Kurtsman slid his chair right in front of Craig's and sat looking at him. He rested his elbows on his knees as he leaned forward to look him in the eye. "Craig, this isn't an instant cure. It will take work and part of that is opening your mind to other possibilities and perspectives. You have done the first step by opening up and sharing with us so we can understand what you're going through. We can't experience your situation but we can empathize with your pain and loss. We are here to support each other as the healing happens. The release of trauma can feel just as painful as the incident itself but unlike the accident, healing from it won't bring recurring pain but instead ways to handle and move past the ache."

"Is it possible to heal from these things?" Rachel asked quietly.

"Yes, it is." Dr. Kurtsman looked at her carefully. "It's difficult but it's possible. There are many side effects that can come along with PTSD such as nightmares and flashbacks, self medicating to numb the pain, and avoidance of anything that reminds us of what we've been through but by facing it and finding coping methods we can take away the power from those things."

The group sat stiffly, looking at him. He didn't know who experienced each of the symptoms he mentioned but he could see in their eyes they all had been through at least one. Craig wiped away the last of his tears. "Let's say we have had some or all of these problems, what do we do about it?"

"We talk about it here. We share out struggles and by letting each other know what we are feeling we can see we aren't alone. When one person finds something that may help with a nightmare or a way to talk about the concern, it can allow someone else to see if that same coping mechanism can assist them in their healing as well. One of the biggest difficulties with PTSD is when we experience a nightmare, a flashback, a panic attack, it feels like we are alone and no one else could ever understand. By talking about it we can see that isn't true. We understand it is a community. You all were victims of terrible situations but sitting in front of each other here you are no longer victims, you are survivors. That is the first mindset we will work on changing."

Dr. Kurtsman looked around to see if what he said hit home with anyone. Craig looked shaky but lighter. The sharing, whether he realized it or not, did help him. Brian and Kyle hadn't looked at each other or said anything since the mention of the common effects of PTSD. The girls sat together watching the rest of the group and he noticed there was a slight change in Jasmine. She looked, calmer somehow, he thought. Rachel had a look on her face of someone who wants to say something but she was so guarded it was hard to tell what it could be.

"Does anyone else want to share anything today?" Dr. Kurtsman asked, suspecting he knew the answer. They all shook their heads. Kyle still had his hand on Craig's shoulder but they didn't seem to notice the connection. Brian stared straight ahead. Jasmine looked like she wanted to escape and Rachel was clutching her now empty bag of chips. "Ok, why don't we call that good for today. I would like you all to think about how you are now survivors and not victims. Next week I would like to have at least a couple of you tell us how that shift in thinking is going."

Without waiting for acknowledgement he got up and put his chair away then began tidying up the kitchen area. That was enough to break the spell. Kyle dropped his arm back to his side as Craig stood up. Brian looked over at Kyle and gestured with a swing of his head in the direction of the door he wanted to leave. Kyle nodded and they headed out, talking in much lower tones than when they had arrived.

Rachel was on her feet but her exaggerated slowness made it clear she was waiting for Jasmine. It took a moment for the older girl to recognize what was happening but when she saw Rachel standing in the middle of the room staring at her she got up and hurried to walk out with her. Craig was taking a long time to put the last few chairs away and watching Dr. Kurtsman as he combined the treats into a single box. "That was quite a meeting."

Dr. Kurtsman met his gaze. There was a small smile below red-rimmed eyes on Craig's face. "How are you feeling?"

"Honestly?" Craig looked at him for a long moment. "Sort of raw. I am glad I was able to share. It's been a really long time since I was able to share my side of things but it brings it all back like it happened yesterday. I have told Caroline, that's my sister, but most of the time she just tries to tell me I shouldn't feel the way I do or tries to fix things. It can't be fixed so I get frustrated and end up hanging up the phone or walking away from her so I don't have to deal with it anymore."

"Have you mentioned any of that to her?" Dr. Kurtsman asked as they walked out the exit. He squinted into the bright sunlight, letting his eyes adjust as he turned to face Craig. "Did you ever try saying, I just need to talk about things. We can work on solutions later but I am hurting and would like to talk about it?"

Craig looked at him. "I guess not. I just get so mad I have to leave the conversation."

"This week, at least once, try talking to her or someone you trust but start out by telling them you aren't looking for a solution. Tell them you are hurting over the loss of your son and would just like to vent and have someone listen. That's all. Just try and talk about it without getting mad. Can you try that for me?"

   Craig nodded, though he looked unsure. Without anything further he turned and walked to his car. Dr. Kurtsman watched him go, giving a quick wave as he pulled away. Craig was right, he reflected, it had been an interesting meeting. He would have liked it if more people had shared but after the intensity of the story today he couldn't blame anyone else for not wanting to take a turn. He knew more stories would be coming, he just hoped they were all strong enough to do the work and start to help one another heal.

# Chapter 4

As Craig pulled out of the parking lot he cracked the window and lit a cigarette. He wanted something a lot stronger but the nicotine would have to do for now to calm his nerves. He hadn't talked about Jeremy that much since he went through the divorce hearings with Patricia and that was only because she had thrown their poor son in his face every chance she got. It was like a mission with that woman to remind him every second that he had caused the worst pain of both their lives and would forever be responsible for all following pain as well.

Craig looked through the windshield, watching the buildings of tiny downtown Clydesburg slip past, slowly transitioning into houses as he moved away from the city center. He turns up the radio and hums along with an old song from his childhood, not heading anywhere in particular, just driving. He knows he should go home and call Caroline like the doc suggested but he didn't feel up for that conversation at the moment. What he wanted more than anything was a drink. He knew that would fall under the self medicating subject they had just heard about but medication was a good thing wasn't it? It helped with the pain.

He took a long drag on the cigarette and watched as the last of the neighborhoods disappeared, spreading out into farmland. The road ahead of him stretched out to the horizon, lined with green fields and pastures. He stubbed out his smoke in the overflowing ashtray, looking down as a few butts fell onto the floor. When he glanced back up he saw a curve ahead in the road and his heart began to race.

His hands involuntarily gripped the wheel so hard his knuckles turned white. He began to shake, ragged breaths coming in bursts. Trickles of sweat ran down his face as he stomped on the brakes at a stop sign just before the curve. Tears jumped into his eyes as the sound from the radio faded and Patricia's voice in his head became all he could hear.

*"Well, I hope you're happy. We can never come here ever again."* She had said.

*"And why is that?" He reminded himself she always calmed down and apologized when she sobered up after a night like this and he just had to weather the storm until she got it out of her system.*

*"You have humiliated me in front of everyone!" She slammed the door as she shrieked the last word. He scanned the nearly empty parking lot. He raised his eyebrows, sweeping his hands around as if to say Everyone? then stared back at her. "Don't be such a condescending prick Craig. You know exactly what you did."*

*"Just get in the car Patty. We need to go home and you need to calm the hell down. You're causing a scene." He climbed behind the wheel before she could respond. He knew she would. There was no way she would tolerate the comment without a long, loud retort, but at least she would have to get in the car to do it.*

*She slammed the door shut as hard as she could and turned to face him. He hooked his thumb under the strap of his seatbelt and her eyes narrowed but she buckled herself in as he hit the power button to start the engine. He reversed quicker than he intended, letting his anger take control for a moment. She grabbed the edge of her seat.*
*"What the hell are you doing?"*

*He didn't respond. He threw the car in drive and peeled out of the parking lot, the force pushing her into the back of her seat. His satisfaction was short-lived as he heard the terrified squeal come from the backseat. Jeremy. He was so frustrated with Patricia and her drama he recklessly forgot he would scare his son as well. He glanced into the wide eyes of his son and silently asked for forgiveness for causing the look he saw reflecting back at him.*

*"You are such an ass." She snapped at him. "You want to celebrate but then won't even let me come up with any fun and enjoyable ways to spend the additional money we are going to have. You get uptight about a drink or two and talk to me like a child."*

*"You're acting like a child." He bit out. Each word clipped as he forced his voice to stay even. "I wanted one nice night with my wonderful son and loving wife. have you seen her, by the way? I would like to talk to her."*

*"Oh go screw yourself Craig." He could feel her stare burning into the side of his head as he focused on the road ahead. "You are such an old man. You don't care about anything exciting. You just want me to be old and boring like you."*

*"We are the same age, Patricia. I like having fun but I want to make sure our house is in good shape, have money set aside for Jeremy to go to college, take care of the things that will make us comfortable when we actually are older. If you had your way we would blow all the money we have traveling around the world and never worry about the future at all. Then one day we would be old and working at some department store living on minimum wage and social security, unable to retire because you had to go through all the money now."*

They had been fighting about money. His promotion would have come with a raise and she wanted to spend it on silly things and not save any of it for the future. He hated that he had to be the grownup all the time but she was always so irresponsible if he didn't act like an old man and force her to do things they would have been broke. He remembered all the times he had to compromise with their wedding plans and the house they bought to keep her within any kind of budget. She had nearly called off the wedding a dozen times because she couldn't get the giant center pieces or the full orchestra to play as she walked down the aisle. She had luxury ambitions and expectations but he made a thrift store salary.

He shuddered as the memory of sliding off the road and bouncing through the field replayed in his mind. Each rut in the ground jarring him to his bones. The tree was ahead but he couldn't get out of the way. The wheel wrenched and twisted out of his hands. When he tried to hold on he felt something pull and snap in his wrist. He had been lucky not to break his arm. When the image reached the point of impact his brain jumped ahead to waking up with flashing lights all around him.

The shadows that had surrounded the car had seemed endless. The police swimming in the midst of strobing lights, the grinding sounds as metal cut into metal when the jaws of life were used, the paramedics rushing him to the waiting ambulance. He remembered Patricia as her head hung limp, held in place by her seatbelt. The vision of the bruise on the side of his face where the airbag had exploded into him floated to the surface. His head ached as he recalled the ringing in his ears and the way everything was spinning. He could feel the ghost of his nausea from that night. The sirens replaced the ringing as his mind carried him to the ambulance and watched the doors slam shut by his feet before the darkness had closed in.

When his mind cleared again he saw himself lying in the hospital, Patricia standing in the doorway, the fires of hatred burning in her eyes. He had been so confused about why she hadn't brought Jeremy to see him. That horrible sarcastic singsong way she spoke to him made him angry even now. Her final words echoing through his heart and soul.

"So I'm selfish?" She spat the words at him. "I only care about myself? You think I don't care about what happens to you or anyone else? This is all about me, is it?"

"Prove me wrong. You came down here knowing I am broken and have been in a medically induced coma for days and yet you didn't even bother to bring Jeremy. He better be with someone safe, by the way. Did it ever occur to you how much it would help to be able to hug my son?"

"Craig, you definitely got worse than I did. I won't argue that for a second. But you didn't get the worst of this by far. Jeremy is definitely with someone safe." She leaned even closer, her lips brushing against his ear. "He is in God's hands now, you bastard. You killed my son."

Rage coursed through him as he tried to smother the memories. The pain lived in him and he felt like it was happening all over again. His vision cleared and the sound of the radio came back as the sound of an impatiently honking horn broke through the past. He glanced in his rearview mirror and saw a man waving his arms emphatically at him. With one final glance at the curve that changed his life forever, Craig turned away and left the ranting driver behind with the memories.

# Chapter 5

Dr. Kurtsman watched from just inside the door as Craig paced back and forth in front of the building. He was chain smoking and had, more than once, taken a quick sip from a flask he pulled from an inner pocket of his jacket. He wanted to go out and see if he could help with the obvious agitation Craig was experiencing but he was weak and needed to stay sitting for the time being. As he looked past Craig he saw Jasmine and Rachel arrive. The girls walked together, slowly, making their way across the parking lot and inside.

Craig stopped long enough to let them go by before resuming his pacing. Dr. Kurtsman noticed as they walked beyond him into the dim interior that both girls had been crying. He wondered what it was about and if either would be willing to open up and talk about it. The girls set up chairs at the far end of the hall in their customary spots and returned to their muted conversation.

After a short time Craig went inside. He saw the girls talking but ignored them. The large, dark bags under his eyes told Dr. Kurtsman all he needed to know about how Craig was doing this week even if he hadn't seen the chain smoking and covert drinking. Dr. Kurtsman carefully made his way down the hall to the chair he set up earlier. On his way he picked up a bottle of water and some crackers. He looked up and saw everyone watching him but thankfully no one said anything. He didn't want to talk about what he was dealing with, he was there to help them.

Just before the meeting officially started Brian and Kyle arrived. Brian walked in first, setting up a chair on the right side of Craig. Kyle followed almost a full minute later, repeating his friend's actions but on the opposite side. When he sat down, staring at the floor Brian folded his arms across his chest and looked around at the rest of the group. Dr. Kurtsman began to stand, felt his body wasn't strong enough to do so, and shifted in the chair instead. He cleared his throat to make sure he had everyone's attention and gave a weak smile when all eyes were on him.

"Welcome everyone, glad to see you and I hope you had a good week." He stopped, taking a deep breath and began coughing so hard he nearly fell out of his chair. He caught himself before he hit the ground but he had to walk his legs around to the side of the chair to stabilize himself. He got himself back under control but was still breathing heavy when he looked up. Rachel was gazing at him with fear and concern radiating from her young face.

"Dr. Kurtsman, what's wrong with you?" She asked, pulling her knees up to her chest the way she had done before.

"What do you mean Rachel?" He tried to sound casual.

"You're breathing hard and coughing really bad. You look super pale and you're drinking water and eating crackers. None of that is like you." The wide-eyed innocence of her made him feel bad but he wasn't ready to talk about things.

"I'll be fine, just a little under the weather today." He could tell from her expression she didn't believe him but thankfully she let it go without any further comment. He looks around and motions for everyone to come closer. "Sorry I am just not able to be as loud as usual today. This silly cough is making it hard."

"Would it be easier to take this week off doc?" Kyle asked.

Dr. Kurtsman shook his head. "No, it'll be fine. I just may need more participation from you all to carry the conversation." He settles back in his chair. "Today I want to make sure anyone that wants to share gets the chance but first I would like to talk about the different ways people handle PTSD."

"You mean like how we all got it?" Brian looked around at everyone then back at Dr. Kurtsman.

"No, there are any number of ways a person could get a diagnosis for PTSD as you are all evidence of. What I want to discuss is coping mechanisms, both good and bad. Last week I mentioned self medicating which is a very common one we see in the medical field. People take prescription pills or start doing drugs, they drink heavily, all in an effort to numb the pain so they don't have to deal with it. That is coping we want to avoid. There are things like the one on one therapy several of you did with Dr. June or support groups like this one that can help. But no matter what you do it is important to also have a strong support network around you, friends and family you can call on when things get particularly rough."

Rachel sighed at the last part but her eyes grew wide and she shrunk into herself when she realized everyone heard her do it. Everyone looked at her, waiting, but she said nothing. Jasmine leaned over and nudged her with an elbow but still the girl sat silent. Dr. Kurtsman made a mental note of the interaction but moved on.

"There are so many who get diagnosed every year but they don't understand it and therefore never learn the right ways to deal with things when an attack arises. They are afraid to ask for help because they believe it is a sign of weakness or others will look down on them." All eyes turned to Brian who sat ramrod straight at the sudden attention. He glared at each person in turn, watching them all back down until his eyes reached Kyle's. There the same contempt and frustration seemed to mirror back at him. The men stared at each other for over a minute until Rachel shifted in her seat, breaking the tension and causing both of them to look over at her.

"Enough of this psycho babble bullshit doc." Brian got to his feet. "You sit there and preach at us but what the hell gives you any right to tell what the right or wrong way to feel is anyway? Do you actually have any experience yourself or is this just crap you learned in books? What have you lost that gives you any ability to lead this group?"

"Why don't you shut up man?" Kyle snapped at him.

"Yeah, all you do is run your mouth but you never contribute anything but you think it's ok for you to question someone trying to help the rest of us? Sit your ass down or get out." Craig agreed.

"Actually I would like to know that too." Eyes widened around the circle as everyone turned to regard Jasmine. "It's hard enough to bare your soul and talk about the worst days of our lives but to do it with someone who leads by reading statistics would be even worse."

Before anyone can go after her for agreeing with Brian, Dr. Kurtsman raised his hands to quiet the group. "It's a valid question. I will admit I have known therapists who run groups that don't have personal experiences with their subject matter and most of their advice does come from what we learn in seminars and statistics we see. I can understand with something so personal how that would be a concern here. As it happens I have had a loss that caused tremendous heartache and put me in therapy." He took a deep breath, sipping water to keep from coughing again. "Several years ago my wife was diagnosed with breath cancer. Shortly after I was given the same diagnosis and we both went into treatment. Mine responded to the chemotherapy but she underwent a mastectomy, chemo and radiation without success. While my cancer went into remission, she lost her battle. I hid from the world. I blamed everyone, including God, for taking my wife away from me. I shut out everything, including my relationship with my son and it has taken years to rebuild what I almost destroyed. So I understand your question and I hope this gives you a better insight into why I am leading this group."

All eyes turned back to Brian who clearly no longer wanted to be the center of attention. He leaned back, mumbling an apology and saying he was sorry about Dr. Kurtsman's wife.

"Thank you Brian." Dr Kurtsman finished his bottle of water.

"It was a reasonable concern. I am hoping to help you all by learning how to share and overcome things as I learned to do in time with my own therapy." He leaned forward, taking in their faces, questions shining in each pair of eyes. He smiled to himself. He felt like he could see the smallest cracks forming in their armor, even Brian. "I could quote statistics at you, let you know currently PTSD affects over seven million people annual. I could tell you that while the majority of them come from the military and while they are the best known group to suffer from the disorder it can come from many situations."

Craig slapped his palms down on his knees. "Is that supposed to be helpful? Is it supposed to make us feel better, or less alone somehow? So what if a bunch of people we don't know and never are going to meet are dealing with their own issues."

"No, not at all. While it's true you aren't alone, all you have to do is look around the room to see that, one of the biggest issues facing people with PTSD is that they feel alone even in a crowd of their peers. There is no cure for that. I know I keep bringing it up but it is important to emphasize. What we can do is figure out what symptoms you each have, what triggers them, and how best to cope with them after that." Everyone shifted, looking around without making eye contact with anyone else.

Finally Rachel looked directly at Dr. Kurtsman. "If it's a disease shouldn't there be some kind of medication that can treat it? And if it is just a bad case of anxiety there should be a way to make it go away."

   Remember, it is called Post Traumatic Stress Disorder. Yes, it triggers anxiety. Usually stronger than anything you have felt before. There are people that get past their trauma and never experience another triggering event but there are just as many, if not more, that spend their lives finding ways to cope with those triggers when they come up. There are medications that can help with the level of anxiety, time can certainly give perspective and help distance you from your individual incidents, and of course, talking about them here can remove some of the power and stigma associated with them. But I want you all to know there is always the possibility that a person, location, or even smell can bring it back and that is when you need to know how to deal with the panic if it floods back in."

   Once again they shared nervous glances and again Rachel broke the silence. "You said last week we should consider ourselves survivors but it sounds like we are always going to be victims."

   "There are always going to be people who say you need to get over your pain. They will say you are playing the victim and looking for attention. I call you survivors because you are here. You are not giving up and by making that choice you are surviving and moving forward." He pushed himself slowly to his feet, holding the back of the chair to steady himself. He began to make his way around the circle, leaning heavily on the chairs as he walked. Between deeps breaths he continued. "You all came together because of Post Traumatic Stress Disorder but perhaps we should reassign those letters to new words, something to do with healing."

   The group fell silent as they thought about it. A few words were tossed out though none of them felt quite right. Brian offered Stupid for the S but quickly apologized after Dr. Kurtsman shot him a dark look. After nearly ten minutes of brainstorming Rachel, who had been quiet up until that point, raised her hand. Everyone turned to her, making her shrink back the way she always did when she was the center of attention. Dr. Kurtsman gestured for her to go ahead. She offered four words. "Perseverance. Trust. Strength. Destiny."

She didn't offer any explanation but to Dr. Kurtsman's astonishment, none seemed to be needed. Everyone kept staring at her for a moment before smiles broke out all around and everyone nodded their agreement. Dr. Kurtsman wasn't sure if they all liked the word choices or they simply recognized how fragile Rachel was but the acceptance made her glow. Dr. Kurtsman sat back down, nodding his own approval. "Now that we have that established, would anyone like to take some time and share about what brought you here?"

Jasmine jumped up. "Actually, while we are focusing on the new words for this evil disorder, maybe we should make some posters or a banner to put them up so when we come in here we can look at the more positive words we chose. I don't have anywhere to go for awhile. If everyone is willing to stick around and help I can even order some pizzas and we can make them this afternoon."

She looked around for support and again Dr. Kurtsman was surprised to see everyone nodding. Even Brian looked like he approved of the arts and craft project. Jasmine pulled out a small notebook and pen from her purse and asked about what they all liked on their pizza. The group all agreed on pepperoni pizzas with a small cheese for Rachel. They listed what sodas they wanted then began discussing the art supplies. That was a more contested conversation.

Craig and Brian both suggested simple white poster board with black or blue markers. Rachel and Jasmine both wanted something more colorful and fun. The tiebreaker fell to Kyle. Brian gave Jasmine a smug look when they realized he would be the deciding vote. Kyle looked at everyone around the circle but his eyes settled on Rachel. He said if it was supposed to be something happy and promote positive thoughts he thought color made more sense. Craig shrugged but Brian's hands instantly curled into fists. Dr. Kurtsman watched as Brian stared down his best friend with an incredulous look.

Dr. Kurtsman hid his smile but he was proud of Kyle. The young man seemed to define himself as Brian's best friend and as a soldier. Both meant doing the expected thing and siding with Brian most, if not all, of the time. Yet here he had gone against the grain and given someone else a win they clearly needed even though it would mean more stress for himself later.

Jasmine smiled as she finished the list of art supplies. Craig and Kyle both offered money to help cover cash and when he saw the other two helping Brian sighed and pulled out his wallet. He handed over some cash, mumbling about hoping things weren't going to be too glittery. Jasmine thanked everyone then bent to grab her purse and keys. Rachel held them out to her as she started walking toward the door. Jasmine looked back at Dr. Kurtsman. He could see she had planned to go alone but it was clear Rachel wasn't going to be left behind. He nodded for her to go and she gave a stiff nod. Jasmine didn't see herself as a role model or mentor but Rachel seemed to and he hoped Jasmine would be able to help her open up.

# Chapter 6

Jasmine led Rachel out to her car, listening to the sound of renewed fighting from behind them. She unlocked the doors as she reflected that it took courage for Kyle to side with them against the other guys, especially Brian. For a brief moment she thought about the fact Kyle could be the type of guy she could actually like. That thought instantly made her shudder however and she tugged at the sleeves of her zippered hoodie. She saw Rachel watching her but said nothing.

They got in the car and Jasmine started the engine. The radio was so loud it made Rachel jump and Jasmine reached over to turn the volume down, apologizing and saying she likes to sing in the car but is tone deaf. Rachel gave her a half smile as she began going through all of Jasmine's preset buttons. She settled on a lite rock station, singing along under her breath. They were about to pull out of the parking lot when a new song came on, a ballad, and Rachel shot up straight, punching the power button with so much force Jasmine yelped. She slammed on the breaks, looking over at Rachel. She couldn't imagine what would make timid little Rachel explode with such a violent reaction.

"What the hell was that about?" Jasmine demanded, turning to look at Rachel. She got no response. Rachel just looked out the window, dragging the sleeve of her sweatshirt across her eyes and under her nose as she stifled a sniffle. "Rachel, look at me. Why did you do that?"

When she still got nothing from her passenger she put the car back in drive and pulled out of the parking lot. She glanced over at the back of Rachel's head. Her heart broke for the girl but her stress was also bubbling up as she drove. She tried a few more times to get Rachel to open up about what caused the reaction but she may as well have been talking to a brick wall. Her hands tightened on the wheel and she turned quickly into a gas station on the right hand side of the road at the last minute. The tires screeched as she slammed on the brakes and threw the car into park. She got out, letting the door close loudly, as she made her way inside. She never looked back at Rachel who watched from the passenger seat, confusion written across her face.

Rachel shifted in the seat, looking into the gas station but she couldn't see Jasmine. She tapped her fingers on the armrest. Her feet moved and readjusted their position in the footwell. She kept glancing toward the building but Jasmine didn't come back out. After what felt like an eternity, Rachel got out of the car and followed Jasmine inside.

She found her with a coffee in her hand, flipping through a magazine. Jasmine didn't look up when she walked in. Instead she continued reading an article and took a long sip from her steaming cup. Rachel opened her mouth to say something but nothing came out. She looked around before taking down a cup and mixing coffee with hot chocolate. She stirred it without drinking. Jasmine glanced at her over the top of the magazine but still said nothing. She, instead, took the cup from Rachel's unprotesting hands and walked to the cashier. There she paid for the drinks and the magazine she had been reading then left Rachel's drink on the counter. She walked out with her own items and got back in the car.

Rachel rushed over to retrieve her drink but followed to the car much more slowly. She reached for the door handle, sure she would be locked out, but it opened with almost no effort. She dropped into the passenger seat once more, staring at the floor. Jasmine started the car and drove off. She didn't ask what was happening with Rachel. She just drove in the direction of the strip mall that had both a craft store and the pizzas they were supposed to pick up.

Rachel played with the lid on her cup but made no effort to drink. She just looked down, watching the steam rise and disappear from the opening. She was so lost in her thoughts she didn't realize

Jasmine stopped again until she heard the door close again. She looked up. Jasmine was walking toward a bench in the park that overlooked downtown. She sat down with her back to Rachel but it didn't feel like she was ignoring her. It felt like she was waiting for Rachel to join her. She wasn't sure she wanted to though. If she went out there she would have to explain herself.

Rachel sat in the car another moment before sighing and walking out to join Jasmine on the bench. She got close but didn't sit immediately. She looked down and saw tears shining in Jasmine's eyes. She reached out a shaking hand, touching Jasmine's shoulder but as soon as she made contact Jasmine jumped away, nearly knocking Rachel's cup from her hands by the intensity of her reaction.

"Jasmine?" Rachel carefully sat on the far side of the bench. "What is going on with you?"

"Why don't you tell me about that song?" Jasmine countered. Rachel looked away. "We are supposed to be sharing what is going on with us, what we feel and why. You nearly punch through my radio but can't tell me about it? Why do you even bother coming to the meetings?"

"You wouldn't understand." Rachel whispers.

"You can't know that without trying to tell me." Jasmine turned to face her. "Look, all I know is I could use a friend and I sort of thought maybe you could too. If I'm wrong tell me and I will leave you alone. I won't try to get you to open up anymore. But I also won't waste any energy trying to help you either. I want to heal and it seems like that is what you want too, or am I wrong?"

Rachel gave a bitter laugh. "Friend? What is a friend?" Jasmine gave her a look but said nothing, waiting for more. "Is a friend someone who guilts you into helping them then turns on you the second someone else spreads a rumor about you? Is it someone who tells lies about you and tells everyone you weren't raped but instead went behind their back and helped their dumb ass boyfriend cheat on them? Is a friend someone who makes everyone you cared about and supposedly cared about you turn against you instead and makes your life miserable until you run away from everyone just to get a moment of peace? Is that what a friend is, because if so I don't need any more of those?"

Jasmine gaped at her. Her tears of frustration now flow from sorrow and empathy. "Is that what happened to you?"

"I wanted to go to a party with some friends from the swim team but my parents are super strict, or at least they used to be when they cared, and they said I couldn't go. I stayed home like I was supposed to and baked a ton of desserts for the church bake sale like my mom told me to but I got a call from my best friend to come pick her up at the party because her boyfriend and her got in a fight. When I got there I couldn't find her and had to go inside. They were fighting and I got a beer thrown on me trying to get her. She took his keys so he wouldn't drive drunk and told me I had to take him home but drop her off first because she was mad at him. I just wanted to get it done and get back before my parents found out I left. I dropped her off and I thought he was drunk and passed out. When we got to his house I helped him into the house but he attacked me. He raped me and then laughed as he took pictures of me running from the house."

"Rachel, oh my God, sweetie." Jasmine wanted to hug her but wasn't sure if she should touch her. Rachel was shaking as the tears fell. "What happened after that?"

Rachel took several deep breaths, trying to get herself under control. "He sent the pictures to my best friend who showed up at my house the next morning screaming at me that I was a slut. She woke everyone up and demanded I explain myself. I tried but she and my parents all blamed me. They told me they couldn't deal with me and stopped talking to me. They barely acknowledge me anymore and won't let me go to church with them or be a part of anything with the family. I stopped going school because everyone was just like Emily and her evil boyfriend. They are still together as far as I know."

It was too much for Jasmine and she pulled Rachel into a tight embrace. They held each other for a few minutes, getting their tears under control before Jasmine let her go. Right at that moment a couple girls in Clydesburg High t-shirts ran by and stopped when they saw them.

"Hey hon," one of them called to Jasmine. "I would watch my back around her if I were you."

"Yeah, especially if you have a man. She likes to steal men, don't you Fish." The second calls with a laugh as they start running off again. Rachel's tears start all over again at the sound of her former nickname.

Between sobs she looked at Jasmine. "Please don't tell anyone what I told you or about what those girls said. I would die if anyone else hated me." She looked around quickly, making sure they were alone again. "Can we get out of here, please?"

Jasmine nodded quickly, helping Rachel to her feet. They got back to the car and headed off to finish their errands. Rachel took the money and list Jasmine gave her and went to the craft store to get everything they needed for the posters while Jasmine went down a few stores to pick up the pizzas. When she got back to the car, Rachel was waiting for her. She set the pizza boxes on top of her trunk, took the bags of supplies and tossed them in the back seat.

Before Rachel could get back in though, she pulled out her phone and put her arm around Rachel's shoulders.

Rachel looked over at her for a second, confused, but then understood. They both did the best they could to smile as Jasmine snapped a few pictures of them together. The tear tracks from earlier were dried and the red noses had faded. On the screen two happy looking faces shone back at them. Jasmine saved the last one as her lock screen on her phone then slipped it back in her pocket and opened the door for Rachel. Once they were in and the pizzas were securely in Rachel's hands, they drove back to the meeting, closer than they had been just an hour ago.

# Chapter 7

"It's about damn time!" Brian explodes when the girls walk through the door. "You have been gone forever, leaving me here with a couple of whiny crybabies and the doc over there who has decided not to talk to me anymore."

Brian jerked a thumb in the direction of Dr. Kurtsman who was sitting near the back wall reading a magazine. He looked up when he heard a reference to himself, nodding at Jasmine. She gave Brian a cool, appraising look. "Well that is your fault. If you didn't spend all your time being such a selfish ass maybe more people would talk to you."

She pushed past him, carrying armfuls of supplies while Rachel followed behind with the food. Dr. Kurtsman smothered a smile as he silently watched Brian try to react to her comments. The other men sat across the room from the kitchen where the girls busied themselves with paper plates and opening the pizza boxes. Rachel came back out to look around for something but seemed unable to locate what she was looking for. She looked back over her shoulder to see if Jasmine was watching but she was digging through the art supplies. Rachel hung her head and hugged herself, staring at the floor as if trying to calm down.

Dr. Kurtsman got up, with considerable effort, his grunting drawing the attention of all the men. He fights for his balance, intending to go over and help Rachel but Brian gets to her first.
"Yo, kid, what is your issue? You look like you saw a ghost or something. Why are you so upset?"

Fresh tears rush into Rachel's eyes and she turns, running into the restroom at the back of the hall, slamming the door behind her. He stood in the middle of the room, watching the spot she had just vacated with a look of wide-eyed innocence on his face. He spread his hands in a "what gives" gesture and looked around at everyone. Jasmine stormed out of the kitchenette and planted herself directly in front of him. She was five inches shorter then he was but the look on her face made him shrink away from her anyway. "Are you kidding me right now? She is the most vulnerable of any of us and you come at her like that? I know you have no concern or consideration for anyone other than yourself but could you at least try to pretend to be a human being for her?"

Brian threw his arms in the air. "Here we go again. The princess is crying and the queen bitch is here to save the day. Guess what, sweetheart, you are no protector. You're just as broken as the rest of us if not more so. Why don't you go set up your arts and crafts project so we can get this over with and get on our way to more productive things in our day?"

Dr. Kurtsman was almost to them by that point. He opened his mouth to give Brian a piece of his mind but a sound like a small thunderclap silenced the room. It took a moment for him to realize what happened. Brian was standing in the middle of the room still, towering over Jasmine who was glaring at him, eyes blazing. His right cheek was already bright red and angry tears slid down Jasmine's cheeks. Kyle rushed past Dr. Kurtsman, inserting himself between them before Jasmine could slap Brian again.

"You hit me." Brian stared at her over Kyle's shoulder. It wasn't lost on Brian that his best friend was standing his ground between them but was facing her.

"You're damn right." The challenge in her voice was unmistakable. "I may not have served in the Army but I am more of a protector than you will ever be."

"Bitch, you are crazy. You're nothing but another crybaby like the rest of this pathetic little group."

"That is enough!" Dr. Kurtsman roared with more force than they had heard from him yet. "Brian you constantly say you don't need this group but you keep showing up. You want the simple truth, I can tell you're scared. You are so afraid everyone here can see through you that you pump up the bravado to hide those insecurities." Jasmine gave Brian a smug look but Dr. Kurtsman turned to her. "Jasmine, you're lashing out. You are just as scared and you are hiding from dealing with your own issues by stepping up to put all of your focus on Rachel and try to protect her in a way I am guessing you weren't."

The smugness disappeared from both of their faces and they turned away from each other. Kyle looked at Dr. Kurtsman in awe. Craig, who up to this point hadn't said anything stood and went to the restroom door. He knocked and quietly asked Rachel to come back out. It took a long time but eventually they all heard the door unlock and she came back into the hall. Jasmine immediately went to her and hugged her hard. She wiped at her cheeks then looked around at everyone, stopping to glare angrily at Brian. He didn't shrink away from her the way he had with Jasmine but he did look away.

Craig walked over to the kitchenette and finished setting out the food Jasmine had been working on then took a few slices of pizza and walked back to his chair. Jasmine looked down into Rachel's face. "He isn't going to say anything like that to you again."

"It wasn't him. I couldn't find the tables to set things up on and all of a sudden I felt like I couldn't breathe. My heart was racing, I felt dizzy and like everything was going out of control. I was sure everyone hated me and I just had to get away."

"No one hates you Rachel." Dr Kurtsman said from a few feet

away. "You had a panic attack. They aren't fun as you can see but they are usually triggered by something and then you have to be able to work through them. That is what I was starting to talk to you all about earlier, coping mechanisms to deal with triggers."

"So that can happen again?" Her look was pure terror.

"I'm sorry to say it's almost a guarantee but I plan to work with all of you to find your triggers and stop them from bothering you as badly. Eventually it may just make you sad for a short while then you will be back to normal." He took a step toward her with the intention to comfort her but thought better of it. "The tables are in the back storage room. Kyle would you help me out and set up a couple so the girls can get everything ready?"

Kyle nodded and followed him to the storage room. Rachel and Jasmine walked together to the kitchenette to get their food and bring out the bags of supplies. Brian followed at a distance, leaving a wide berth for Rachel when he picked up his pizza and a soda. After they got the tables set up, Kyle and Dr. Kurtsman helped themselves to food as well.

They ate in silence then started in on the posters. Craig spelled out each word in block letters on different sheets of poster board. He then handed one to Kyle and Brian who began to paint the letters with the bold colors the girls had picked out. Jasmine and Rachel started on another, making generous use of the glitter. Dr. Kurtsman worked on another with Craig creating the last one himself.

As they worked, Jasmine would periodically get up and walk around the group taking pictures. Brian mumbled something under his breath but Kyle would nudge him and he would get back to work. It took hours to complete the project which seemed to make Rachel very happy. When they finished and all of the posters were lined up on the table to dry she stood looking at them. Jasmine came up beside her and squeezed her hand. "This was a great idea Rach. Now when we come in we will see these signs of hope and healing. If we are struggling we can look up at the words and know what to focus on."

Dr. Kurtsman watched as Rachel looked around at everyone. He could see they were all exhausted, emotionally wrought, and glad to be done. They were all also smiling. Even Brian looked proud of what had been created. Rachel seemed to be staring at the last two posters. "I think you're right Jasmine. I think this project has given me the strength to follow my destiny and do what I have to in order to finally feel better."

# Chapter 8

Rachel walked into her house. The sound of the door closing and the lock engaging seemed to echo in the house. She was alone. Usually her parents would be there but at the moment the solitude was peaceful. She leaned against the counter staring at the kitchen. She had spent hours in here cooking with her mom back when her parents still included her as part of the family. She had learned to cook and bake in this room. In fact, her mind forced her to remember, she had been baking various treats for the church bake sale the night everything went wrong.

She pushed herself away from the counter and walked through the lower level of her house. She touched some of the knickknacks her mother collected and picked up a few pictures of her parents her father always kept out on the side table. With a sigh, and a last look around, she made her way up to her room. It had been a long day. She closed the door, leaning back with a yawn and heard the sound of the car pulling into the drive. She had hoped they would be out longer but it didn't matter, they never talked to her anymore anyway. She listened for the sounds of her parents coming in and settling down to watch a television program or read. She waited, breath held for a few minutes but it didn't take long to know they weren't coming to check on her.

She dropped onto the foot of her bed. Her foot kicked a book on the floor and she bent to see which one it was. She saw she held a text book from one of her classes she had been enrolled in when she was still attending school. She hadn't officially dropped out but no one cared if she went to class or not and she had no desire to put herself through that experience again. She stood up, flipping through the pages, trying to remember what the story had been about. Without looking where she was going she walked into her desk chair, knocking it over with a crash.

Seconds later she heard footsteps rushing up the stairs then her father pounding on her door. "I'm sorry, it was an accident."

"Yes, I'm sure it was. Nothing is ever your fault is it?" Sarcasm dripped from his words. "You better not be making a mess in there, or doing anything to bring more shame to this family."

With that the footsteps retreated back down the stairs. Rachel could hear her parent's muffled voices talking below her. She let out a breath she hadn't realized she was holding and forced back the tears threatening to fall. She sinks to the floor next to the fallen chair, taking deep breaths and praying for strength.

When she was sure the tears would stay at bay she put the chair quietly back in place. She got up, sliding onto the seat and pulled a few empty pages from a notebook. With a long sigh she began writing. She knew what she wanted to say and to whom but her hands shook as each word was scrawled across the pages. The tears began to sting the corners of her eyes again as she neared the end of the message. She folded up the pages before stuffing them into an envelope then printed the name on the front.

She dropped it on her bed as she walked by on the way to her closet. Rachel pulled her swim jacket with the hateful nickname on the back off the hanger and smashed it into the trashcan in the bathroom. She filled a glass of water and took down her bottle of aspirin, taking a large handful of pills a few at a time. She looked at her reflection for a moment while waiting to make sure she wouldn't throw up the pills. Then, before her determination failed her, she pulled apart her razor. She dragged the edge of the blade from her wrist up her arm nearly to the elbow, first on one arm then the other. The blood ran down her arms, splattering on the floor and counter, making the mess she had specifically been told not to create. Her reflection smiled back at her as she realized she didn't care.

Rachel made her way back to the bed, lying against the pillows.

She pulled the letter close and picked up a white rose Jasmine had given her at the park earlier. She watched as the blood continued to pour out, draining the life from her body. The world began darkening at the edges so she closed her eyes. She whispered goodbye to Jasmine, Dr. Kurtsman, and anyone else who might have actually cared about her. She begged God to forgive her for what she had to do but she couldn't hurt anymore. Relief flooded through her body at the thought and as a single tear escaped her closed eyes Rachel Morris's pain and life ended.

# Chapter 9

Jasmine tossed and turned when she went to bed. She couldn't shake the feeling something was wrong but after the meeting everything had seemed to be heading in a good direction. They agreed on the words, she stood up to Brian which had felt incredible, and Rachel had been so happy with what they created. So what was bugging her? She didn't know.

She watched some shows and infomercials during the early hours of the morning then when the sun came up she went out to take some pictures. She always liked the dawn, the colors brushing the horizon like a divine paintbrush. It was the perfect time of day to meditate and think about new beginnings in the day and in life. Dr. Kurtsman was right about needing to redefine the words so they could be something positive instead of a dire mental illness. She hoped everyone else thought that way too. She walked around her neighborhood snapping pictures of gardens and the scenery as the sun took a low position in the morning sky.

As she made her way back she stopped in her mother's garden and picked a white rose. She smiled at it as she thought about the one she had given Rachel the day before. She pushed open the back door to the kitchen, smelling the coffee now brewing inside. It was intoxicating. Her mother was sitting at the table with a cup in front of her already, reading the paper. Jasmine walked in, heading for the coffee maker when a headline on the front page stopped her cold. *Teen Found Dead Of Apparent Suicide* it screamed at her. The rose fell from her hand, tumbling to the floor. She didn't have to read any further, she knew who the teen was.

Jasmine dropped to her knees with a thud causing her mother to toss aside the paper and rush over to her. Georgia Byers looked at her daughter with grave concern. "Jas, what's wrong?"

Jasmine tried to respond but the words failed her. She shook her head hard, trying to shake away the image of the headline but it remained, suspended in the vision behind her eyelids. When she finally got herself under some kind of control again, she climbed to her feet and picked up the discarded paper. She read the entire article twice, not fully believing it the first time through. She looked back at where her mother had retaken her chair. "This is the girl from my support group. The one I was becoming friends with. She killed herself last night."

Georgia took the paper and folded it on the table then wrapped Jasmine's hands in her own. "Honey, I'm so sorry. Did you have any idea she would do something like that?"

Jasmine stared dully at her mom. "No. In fact yesterday was the first time she seemed kind of happy and at peace. She was talking about being strong enough to follow her destiny and feel better." Jasmine's eyes widened as it struck her. "This is what she meant. She was telling us she was strong enough to kill herself to stop hurting."

The sobs shook her entire body as despair flooded through Jasmine. She nearly fell, Georgia caught her and helped her into the closest chair, then brought her some water. She continued to cry until it felt like there was nothing left inside her. When it passed once more Jasmine pulled the paper to her and read through the article a third time. Then she got up, grabbed her car keys and purse and headed for the door.

"Where are you going?" Georgia asked, confused.

"I need to go to Rachel's house. The support group were her friends and I am sure her family is struggling right now. The least is can do it try and help them." She didn't wait for a response. She ran the short distance to the car and slid behind the wheel. It didn't take long to drive the several blocks to Rachel's street and she saw there were a number of cars in front of the address listed in the paper. Others paying their respects to the family, Jasmine thought as she parked at the end of the block. She walked down to the house and knocked on the door, itching to hug the parents of the girl she cared so much about.

After the second knock a matronly woman answered the door. The red rimmed eyes and flushed cheeks told Jasmine all she needed to know, this was Rachel's mother. She looked completely distraught. Behind her stood a man who looked like someone sucker punched him in the gut. Her parents were devastated. How could Rachel have not seen that they cared for her so deeply?

"Can we help you?" The woman asked in a hoarse voice.

"I'm sorry to intrude. I saw the news and watched to pay my respects and condolences." Jasmine began.

The woman burst into tears. "Thank you for coming in our time of need. Please come in."

"Thank you." Jasmine entered and followed the couple into the living room. They sat together on the sofa and she could see a few others milling about in the house. Her heart broke as she watched them holding each other. Gently, Jasmine lowered herself onto the edge of a chair across from them.

"Can you believe she would do this?" Rachel's father asked. Jasmine shook her head, wiping at tears. "It is just so shameful."

Shameful? Jasmine was taken aback by the choice of words. "It's a tragedy."

"She just never thought about how all of this would affect us." Her mother wailed. "She made a terrible mess up there and then to bring all of this horrible attention to the family as though she didn't embarrass us enough with her antics months ago."

Jasmine was speechless. She stared at the couple rocking back and forth in the grief they apparently only held for the loss of their reputations. She felt ashamed now of thinking Rachel could have misjudged how her parents felt about her when clearly they were nothing more than narcissistic monsters. She looked from one to the other, mouth hanging open but nothing coming out. She was about to get up when someone approached from the kitchen and asked about a memorial service. Rachel's mother sighed and said since people kept asking they probably should.

"I would very much like to come to the service and show my support." Jasmine said.

Rachel's father focused back on her as though he had forgotten she was there. "What did you say your name was again?"

"I actually didn't say, it's Jasmine Byers."

"You're Jasmine?" Her mother's face darkened instantly. Jasmine nodded and watched as her mother got up and stalked to the kitchen. She returned a few seconds later with a letter in her hand and threw it at Jasmine. "This is your fault. You and that group of yours. You brain washed her and put this wretched idea in her head. Now she has gone and brought humiliation on our home again. We will have to move in order to escape the shame, if we can ever sell the house. Get out, you are not welcome here."

The final part was spoken through tightly gritted teeth. Jasmine picked up the letter which had fallen at her feet. She saw her name written on the front of the envelope and the pages of notebook paper stuffed haphazardly inside. She assumed Rachel's parents had read the letter but she didn't care. These words were for her and she would read and care for them. She didn't understand what had happened but she could see this was not a loving home with people needing help, it was a house of horrors that Rachel had somehow survived until last night. She stood, turned on her heel, and stomped out the door.

When she got home she read the letter. It was obvious Rachel had been fighting every painful memory and emotion when she wrote it from the shaky handwriting to the hurried words, many of which were misspelled. But they were hers. Jasmine hugged the pages to her chest and cried for the life lost and the girl who never had a chance.

Two days later there was a memorial service at Rachel's parent's church. Jasmine waited until the service was about to start then snuck in and sat in the back. She saw many of the people who had been at the house when she went over to try and comfort people who couldn't have cared less. Close to the front was a group of girls wearing matching jackets. Jasmine could see one just like it hanging up in front. Even from where she sat near the doors in the back she could see the nickname embroidered on the back, Fish.

The pastor got up and welcomed everyone. He said it would be a short service to allow the family to grieve in peace and privacy. Jasmine almost snorted at the mention of the family grieving. If they were, it wasn't for their daughter. Mrs. Morris got up and hugged the pastor before taking her place at the podium.

"Thank you all for coming. As you can imagine, this has been a terribly hard time for us and we appreciate you being here as we struggle through it. Rachel was a troubled girl and many of you know about her unfortunate indiscretion several months ago. We are so ashamed she did that and blame ourselves for not getting her the help she so clearly needed before she felt the need to act out. Her friends from the swim team are here as well and I am so happy to see your faces, I'm sorry she ruined the end of your season with her behavior."

She stopped to take a sip of water and Jasmine felt herself shaking. Her hands clenched and unclenched as she listened to the self serving lies of Rachel's mother. She muttered to herself under her breath.
"Bitch."

"We have decided against a eulogy and instead will simply ask for a few moments of silence. After the service there will be a small gathering in the reception hall downstairs where everyone can come together and share their feelings."

With that her father came up, stood stoically by his wife for a moment then led her back to the front row. Jasmine's rage overwhelmed her and she stood up. She walked to the front and took her place behind the podium now vacated by Rachel's mother. She looked at the gathered faces, all staring back at her in confusion and concern.

"My name is Jasmine Byers and I was a true friend of Rachel's. She was a wonderful girl who wanted to live and make a difference more than anything. She talked about it in our support group even though she was afraid. She suffered from PTSD and I am willing to bet the person that gave it to her is in this room. Rachel was raped a few months ago, that is what her mother calls "acting out" and I think the only shameful thing is your behavior. You treat your own daughter like dirt and expect people to feel bad for you. They might, but I don't. You accused the group of causing Rachel's suicide but she came to us for help and support because you couldn't be bothered to act like a human being and love her. You blamed her for something that wasn't her fault at all and drove her into the ground, literally."

At that point Rachel's father stood up. "How dare you?"

"How dare I? No sir, you have that backwards. How dare you stand up here with your wife and act like the victims. Rachel was the victim and it was perpetrated by all of you. She was broken and instead of helping stitch her back together, you shredded what was left. She was a beautiful soul and a wonderful friend. You killed her and I hope you can live with that." Jasmine walked away from the podium. She stopped to pull down the swim jacket hanging up and took it with her, throwing it in the trash when she got to the back. The congregation stared at her as she walked calmly down the main aisle and out through the main door.

She heard the room explode into chatter when she left but she didn't care. She drove to the park, sitting at the same bench she and Rachel had shared just days before. As she looked out over the downtown buildings she heard the sound of approaching footsteps. She looked over she shoulder and saw a girl even younger than Rachel watching her. "Who are you?"

"My name is Mandy." The girl edged closer until she was standing in front of the bench. Jasmine gestured for her to sit down but Mandy shook her head. She was playing with her purse strap and shifting from one foot to the other. "I feel weird telling you this but I followed you from the memorial, or whatever that was supposed to be."

Jasmine smiled at that. "It was a joke is what it was."

Mandy nodded, solemnly. "I was on the swim team with Rachel before she quit. I know what happened between her and Emily and Emily's boyfriend Danny. She told us he raped her but Emily accused her of going behind her back and seducing him. Rachel was torn up about it. She quit the team and left school. I always wanted her to know I believed her but I knew if I spoke up it would be just as bad for me. I never thought she would do something like this. I wish I would have said something."

Jasmine's smile disappeared instantly. "You believed her but never said anything?"

"I wanted to. I was just scared. It's so sad what happened and if I could go back I would definitely do something, she was my friend."

"Some friend, you could have defended her but never bothered. You were so worried about yourself you didn't do something as simple as telling her you believed her and she wasn't alone. That could have made all the difference in the world to know someone was on her side. With friends like you no wonder she is gone." Jasmine folded her arms across her chest and turned away, tears streaking down her cheeks again. Mandy began to cry as well and turned, fleeing back to the parking lot. She ran past Kyle as he approached the bench.

"That was kind of harsh, don't you think?" She turned to look at him through her swollen eyes. "She was trying to share her feelings and you ate her alive. She was just trying to share what a shame this all is."

"It isn't a shame, what happened to Rachel is a tragedy." She glared at him. "And she didn't do a damn thing even though she was in a position to stand up to those girls who bullied Rachel."

Kyle held up his hands in surrender. She continued through her tears asking how anyone could turn their backs like Rachel's parent's did, especially on someone like her. He shakes his head, looking over at her. He tells her the group was there for Rachel and never turned their backs on her, especially Jasmine. He tells her she would be proud of what an amazing friend she had been to someone who needed it so badly.

"If I was so great, why did she leave us? Why did she leave our little family?" She crumbled into his arms as the tears came full force. He stiffened, knowing her previous reactions to men touching her but she seemed oblivious so he held her until her sobs were under control. Then she sat up again and looked at him. "What are you doing here?"

"We all went to the funeral. Craig, Dr. Kurtsman, Brian, and I were there but you didn't see us. You were too focused on taking care of the parents, good job by the way. Even Brian wanted to punch them. When you stormed out we came after you. I remembered hearing you and Rachel talk about your detour here when we were making the posters so when we couldn't keep up with you in traffic I figured this was a safe bet on where you were heading."

Jasmine looked over his shoulder and saw the rest of the group in the parking lot. Dr. Kurtsman was talking to Mandy while Brian and Craig did their best not to be a part of anything. "I just can't believe she is gone, that she killed herself."

"I'm just glad you never thought about doing something like that." He told her.

She looked away from him. "Actually I did once."

"You're joking right? You are far too strong and smart to do something like that."

"I'm not strong but I was even weaker once. I wanted to die more than anything."

"Jasmine, it isn't funny to joke about things like that."

Her eyes flashed as she looked at him. "They are burying someone I love as we speak, why the hell would I joke about it?"

He gave her an appraising look. She had on a black pantsuit with long sleeves and a fitted black top under the jacket. There were no visible marks he could see but then he realized she always wore long pants and long sleeves. "Do you have scars from the attempt?"

"I have plenty of scars but not from that. I was going to take all of my parent's sleeping pills and wash it down with liquor from their liquor cabinet. You want to know what stopped me?" He nodded but she could see the uncertainty in his eyes. "I was afraid I would screw it up. My ex-boyfriend's voice was in my head telling me I didn't deserve to live but it also told me if I tried to kill myself I would mess up and just be a bigger disappointment and embarrassment than I already was. It nearly killed me and it saved my life, that voice."

"Well, it doesn't matter what saved you. You're here and healing. You come to group and help others. I hope you don't think about it anymore."

"No, not anymore. At least not until Rachel died and abandoned me. You say I am helping people but I wasn't strong enough to help her." He tried to reach out to hold her again but she pushed him away. Instead she wrapped her arms around herself as the tears began to flow once more. She shivered as she thought about the coldness from Rachel's parents, her so-called friends blaming her for her own rape and bullying her. She thought about the letter and the white rose her parents said she had been holding. Jasmine had given her the white rose earlier that day. Her parents had been appalled she would use a symbol of purity in her suicide but the letter had said it was for the group. She wanted them to keep fighting and healing; she just couldn't stay.

"We are a family," Kyle whispered from the other side of the bench. As though he had read the letter himself he assured her.
"Rachel would want us to keep fighting."

She pulled out her phone and looked at the picture she had taken with Rachel. "She was a beautiful spirit."

"She still is and she is watching over us, all of us. We need to stick together and do our best to heal for her. We need to make her proud and help everyone we can to get better so no one has to hurt the way she did ever again."

Jasmine looked at him then back at the parking lot again. Everyone was leaning on Dr. Kurtsman's car, looking at the two of them on the bench. Standing next to Dr. Kurtsman was Mandy, looking like she desperately needed a friend.

# Chapter 10

When he got home from the funeral, Dr. Kurtsman sat at his dining room table and pulled out the notebook he kept with thoughts from each meeting and about each of the members. He always had notes on his patients in their files when he was still practicing and it was second nature to continue now. He took a sip of water, washing down some of his pills, and flipped through the pages. The first on his list was Craig Stillwell.

It was easy to see the survivor's guilt was eating him alive inside. He also had a problem with drinking. The biggest concern was he was keeping it a secret, or at least thought he was. The smell of the alcohol was noticeable and Dr. Kurtsman had seen him sneak whiskey into his coffee more than once before the meetings. Drinking was a common coping mechanism for someone going through a loss such as his but it was self destructive and could easily spin way out of control.

Craig had invited Kyle, Brian, and Dr. Kurtsman out for a drink at the bar after they left the park but the other men refused. Craig shrugged it off but the look in his eyes had been a mix of disappointment and fear. Dr. Kurtsman had no doubt Craig knew how dangerous the line he was walking could be but felt sure he didn't know how to get off that path and back on solid ground.

The next page contained information and observations about Brian Nickerson. Narcissistic to a fault, he was the biggest challenge in the group. The bravado he spoke with and blatant aggressive behavior were classic signs of a deep inferiority complex. He believed he was destined to be a great leader but he self-sabotaged every opportunity that came his way. He refused to follow directions, claiming he knew a better way but ultimately he was afraid of being in charge because if things went to hell he would have no one to blame but himself and he couldn't allow himself to be seen as wrong.

They had touched on the situation that happened oversees and he knew Brian had instigated the problem by taking charge over Kyle and ignoring orders to stand down. But because there were others above him, he was able to lay the blame at their feet, shielding his fractured ego. He wanted to be seen as in charge without having to actually do the work so he never allowed others to teach him or lead him. He didn't want to come across as a follower or weak but because of that, he destroyed any real strength he possessed and became a liability.

Kyle Masters was the complete opposite. A natural born leader, he had no desire or ambition to be in charge. From the brief one on one moments they had had, he knew Kyle grew up in the foster care system. When he was young he moved in down the street from Brian and his family and had been symbolically adopted. Brian's father was an Army man to the core and shoved it down the throats of the boys. Kyle deferred to Brian the whole time they were growing up and even now when he was clearly the more stable one with insight, and a strong moral compass, he fell back into his habit of following Brian.

That secondary role he played so naturally made it difficult for him to stand up to Brian when he got out of line, though there had been flashes of his inner strength a few times. What blew Dr. Kurtsman away was Kyle's compassion. He had moved to comfort Craig when he broke down over the accident and loss of his son. He had been the one to go speak to Jasmine in the park, and there was obviously a connection between them. Dr. Kurtsman wasn't sure if it was romantic or more of a sibling type relationship but there was a closeness he had seen developing slowly between them. He made a note to keep an eye on that as well.

Jasmine Byers was a difficult study. She had been a closed book when it came to her trauma. She said it was an abusive relationship but that was all. In fact, she had only admitted it was a relationship that ended badly, but her behavior was text book for someone who had been manipulated and controlled. She blamed herself for anything having to do with her but was quick to sacrifice herself for anyone else she thought was about to get hurt. She had a strong distrust of men in general but had been fiercely protective of Rachel.

The thought of the youngest member of the group made Dr. Kurtsman put down his pen and wipe tears away from his eyes. Rachel Morris had been through hell. Not only did the rape destroy her physically and emotionally, but the lack of support from anyone outside the group ruined any chance of her recovery. His heart broke as he remembered the words in the letter she wrote for Jasmine and the rest of the group.

All Rachel wanted was a place to belong and people who loved her. She lost the sport her world had revolved around; her friends became enemies and predators overnight. The part that made him sick the most was her parents. When they welcomed people to the church for the service her mother had thanked everyone for taking the time and apologized for them having to put up with Rachel's "overly dramatic behavior". Dr. Kurtsman's hands had balled into fists immediately and he had to fight the deep urge to punch her father in the face. Kyle and Craig had similar reactions and even Brian had stared at them with his jaw hanging open.

When he heard them talking about how they had done everything they could and had no idea why she felt the need to bring such disgrace to the family he had brushed past into the church without speaking because he knew he wouldn't be able to hold his tongue. The other men had followed him with nearly identical looks of disgust then they all stopped short when they realized just how few people were in attendance. Mostly it was people supporting her parents, no one was paying attention to her.

There was a gaggle of girls in swim jackets matching the one hanging in front that Jasmine would later remove on her way out.

They had stood together laughing as though they were at a party instead of a funeral. The only one who showed any concern, even in the church she had looked out of place with the others, was Mandy.

He had been impressed by her determination and bravery to follow Jasmine and talk to her in the park. He was also grateful Jasmine's emotional explosion hadn't completely scared her off. The girl had stayed and spoken with him in the parking lot of the park while Kyle did his best to comfort Jasmine. He had offered Mandy the opportunity to come and talk about what she was feeling at their meetings. She had been non-committal but he hoped she would decided to come at least once.

He closed the notebook, setting his pen aside. He looked up at the picture of his wife staring back at him. He reached out, gently picking it up as though he was holding her in his hands instead of a pewter frame. Hugging it tight he felt a few tears of his own escape. He missed her terribly but as he held her image he saw the medical folder on the edge of the table and realized he might be closer to her than he wanted to admit. He closed his eyes as the words from his most recent doctor appointment echoed in his mind. "I'm sorry James, the cancer is back and is far more aggressive this time. It has already metastasized in several areas making surgery impossible. We can try chemo to slow it down but at this time there is little else we can do. If things continue to progress at the current speed, my best guess is you have a little less than a year left."

# Chapter 11

Craig sat on the bar stool staring at his beer and shot of whiskey. He had ordered them as soon as he walked in but for the first time in months, he didn't want a drink. As he stared at the amber liquid in front of him he remembered the blackout he experienced the night Patricia filed for divorce. That thought flowed into the hazy memory of the bender he had gone on after Jeremy died. He had taken almost all of his pain killers and drank all the beer he had in the house. He had wanted to die and be with his son again. He woke up three days later with a police office shaking him back to consciousness on a park bench in another town. To this day he had no idea how he ended up there.

He drank almost daily, though he was loath to admit that to anyone, but it wasn't numbing the pain the way it used to. He thought about Dr. Kurtsman discussing coping mechanisms and how some of them could be just as harmful as what they were being used to treat. When he first came home from the hospital he used the pain killers then added the alcohol later. His sister, Caroline, was there when he battled that particular demon. She fought him and won as she got him past that growing addiction. The drinking was different. He did his best to keep it from her and though he was sure she knew about it either she didn't realize the extent or it was one war she didn't have the energy to wage on his behalf. When she went back to her own house the consumption increased and he didn't bother hiding it. Within a few weeks he was traveling everywhere with the flask Dr. Kurtsman had seen so he could add a little flavor to things like coffee.

But as he sat there, not drinking, he wasn't thinking about his divorce, his lost job, his sister, or even the pain of losing his son. He was thinking about Rachel and her pain. He hated himself for not seeing it sooner. He was a father and this child had been in front of him the whole time but he was so focused on his own grief he was blind to how much she was hurting.

He pulled out his phone, opening the photo gallery, to look at pictures of Jeremy smiling his mischievous grin that had always melted his heart. He wondered what Rachel had looked like when she was his age. He would have bet his life savings she was just as adorable back then, back when she was still whole and the apple of her parent's eye. Now she was buried in the ground, like Jeremy.

His mind flashed back to Jeremy's funeral. He saw Patricia standing with him as they took their positions next to a grave where an obscenely small casket sat up on risers. They supported each other as people paid their respects but as soon as they were alone she had given him a manila envelope then stormed off. As the tires from the car screeched away he had opened it to find she served him with divorce papers. She had been as cold as Rachel's parents earlier that day. It sent a shiver through him.

He wished he could talk to Rachel right now. He thought about all the times at the meetings he could have asked how she was doing, or offered to set up her chair for her. He could have at least asked how school was going or said anything to show her someone cared. She was young enough to be his kid, but somehow that made his lack of action hurt even worse.

He reached for the now warm beer but instead of drinking it he placed some bills under the bottle and stood up. Jeremy's memory deserved better than this and so did Rachel's. She would never get the chance to heal but he was going to heal for her. He closed the photo gallery and opened a search, looking for the closest Alcoholics Anonymous meeting. There was one starting in half an hour at the church near his house. If he left right away he could make it.

He could get there faster if he drove past the curve where the accident had happened but he wasn't ready for that yet. He sat in his car, asking himself if he really was ready for this but the image of

Rachel smiling at the posters at their last meeting floated into his mind and he put the car in drive.

He got to the church with just a few minutes to spare before the meeting started. He watched people filing into the basement. Taking a deep breath, he followed them. He knew he had a long journey ahead of him and the guilt was immense. As he entered the room he silently thanked Dr. Kurtsman for his guidance. He still believed there was no one else he could blame for the accident but he also trusted it was not completely his fault. He needed a new start and hopefully this was a place he could find it.

Craig stood in the back of the room, watching everyone as they gathered snacks and drinks then sat down to begin. He edged to a seat in the back row, much the way Rachel had come into their first meeting, and faced the podium and the speaker took their place. People got up and shared how their week had been going, triumphs and pitfalls, and after several gave updates the meeting leader asked if there was anyone new who would like to share.

Swallowing his fears, Craig raised his hand. He was gestured to the front and slowly made his way forward. He faced the crowd of relative strangers, trying to figure out what to say. "I know everyone has to hit rock bottom before they are ready to make a change. I didn't get drunk enough to start a fight or get arrested for drunk and disorderly. I didn't lose my home or anything like that. It has been a long several months starting with an accident that killed my four year old son when I was driving, and no I wasn't drunk at the time. My wife was and she and I got into a fight. I lost control of the car and we slammed into a tree. She and I lived but my baby didn't make it. She blamed me and filed for divorce. That is when I started drinking. My sister pushed me into therapy, which I thought would be a bunch of crap but he diagnosed me with PTSD and I started going to a support group for that as well. I have still been drinking everyday but today I sat in a bar with a beer and a shot in front of me and I didn't want them. There was something that opened my eyes when nothing else seemed to work. If it's ok I want to take a few minutes and tell you about that reason. Her name was Rachel."

# Chapter 12

Dr. Kurtsman stood in the corner, letting the shadows close around him. He wasn't hiding exactly, he was simply observing. He sipped his water, swallowing more of his pills while he waited. Craig was first as usual. He came in through the door, stopped for a minute to let his eyes adjust to the dimmer light then began to make his way to the end of the hall where they met.

Usually he would come straight down, set up his chair, then get a coffee with his added flavoring and wait for everyone else. Today was different. He made it halfway down when he stopped dead in his tracks. His breathing quickened and a hand came up involuntarily to his chest, covering his heart. Craig's knees started shaking and he had to lean against the wall to keep from falling over. His tears fell in torrents as he sobbed loudly. Dr. Kurtsman watched all of this from his spot at the end of the hall. He knew Craig was reacting to the circle of six chairs set up and the posters they had made the previous meeting being up on the wall.

It took over a minute for Craig to get himself under control. When he did he finished walking down to the end of the room. He walked to the kitchenette but there was nothing waiting for him there. He shot Dr. Kurtsman a questioning glance but he had more pressing things on his mind. "Why would you do that doc? Don't you think it is way too soon to put up the posters? Those were Rachel's words. She chose them and we all know that. I guess I can understand setting out a chair for her but the posters, that's just wrong."

"I didn't do it." Dr. Kurtsman shrugged.

"And why are you standing in her spot? She hid in the corner at the beginning of that first meeting. Are you trying to channel her or something?"

"Honestly, I'm just trying to stay out of the way. None of this was my doing." Before either could say anything further, another voice cuts through the air.

"Are you kidding me with this?" Brian bellows from the far end of the room. "How exactly did you think it was a good idea to shove these posters in our face today?"

He kicked at the chipped tile he tripped over before as he made his way down to the other men. Dr. Kurtsman raised his hands in surrender and Craig shook his head. "It wasn't us man. I just got here myself."

Brian looked around again. He glared at the sparkling posters hanging on the wall then turned on the circle, counting the six chairs waiting patiently for people to fill them. Craig and Dr. Kurtsman watched as his eyes flicked back and forth between the two offending situations. After awhile he shook his head in an exact imitation of Craig. When he looked back at them his face was a mask of confusion and frustration. He looked over at the kitchen but he saw the same thing Craig had, there was no coffee, no refreshments at al, waiting for them. He balled his fists, preparing to go off on another tangent when he was interrupted the same way he had invaded Craig and Dr. Kurtsman's conversation.

"What are the posters doing up?" Kyle's voice shook as he approached. He saw the men gathered in the corner. They were all looking at him with different expressions. Dr. Kurtsman simply appeared to be observing while Craig's eyes told him he felt the same way. Brian, on the other hand, was giving him a venomous glare.

"Well, nice of you to join us. I had to get a ride here since my car still isn't working and every time you are supposed to come over and help you find some excuse to bail on me. Where were you this morning?" Brian spat the words.

I took Riveria back to the airport. I told you I was doing that. It was nice of him to come back here and hang out for a couple days after Arlington. You should have spent more time with him. He is the only other one that made it and he has been doing really well. It might have been good for you guys to talk." Kyle said as he walked over to join the group.

"I'm sure he is doing great, why wouldn't he be perfect?" Brian rolled his eyes.

"He went through the same things we did. Get your head out of your ass and maybe you will see others around you are hurting too." Kyle held up a hand to silence Brian. "I know, I know. You're going to say you aren't hurt. You're fine and the world needs to get over things and stop crying about it. You can always go home and work on the piece of crap car of yours but I need to be here so just don't, ok?"

"Arlington?" Craig asked.

Kyle cut his eyes to look at the other man. He gave a slight nod, turning to face him squarely. "Yes, the day after Rachel's funeral we flew out to attend the memorial services for the fallen members of our team that died in the firefight. They are buried in Arlington National Cemetery. They were buried already but because of the size of the group they did the formal ceremony for all of them together and it was this past week. Rafael Riveria was the other surviving member of our group and he came back here for a couple days after we left Arlington."

"And apparently he is doing just fine, proving this PTSD bullshit isn't real." Brian snapped back at him.

"Not everyone is affected the same way by the same situations Brian." Dr. Kurtsman cut in. "Two people can go through the same experiences and have completely opposite reactions. That's human nature, not everyone will have the same concerns or lack thereof."

They all started talking at once, attempting to make their own opinions heard above the din. None of them noticed Jasmine enter, carrying a large coffee container and a box of donuts balanced on top. She made it almost the entire way to the kitchen when she stumbled. Kyle saw her just in time and reached out, catching the sliding box of donuts before it fell to the floor. She looked up and gave him a grateful smile then finished taking the coffee in and setting it on the kitchen counter. She then came back out to retrieve the box but Kyle held it away from her. The look on his face was of grave concern but she just smiled and snatched the box back and set it on the counter next to the coffee.

She got a cup of coffee, sniffing the fragrance with satisfaction. She walked to the wall, pressing one of the posters more securely in place then walked over to take her seat. She looked at the men expectantly, the smile still plastered on her face.

Brian and Kyle both got drinks and donuts then sat down. Kyle took a long look at Jasmine, studying her for a minute. Brian and Dr. Kurtsman watched him watching her. She knew he was looking at her but seemed to be refusing to acknowledge it. However she tugged at her sleeves, massaging her right wrist briefly then hugged herself. Her right had lightly rubbed back and forth over her left shoulder. She stared straight ahead though, and her smile stayed frozen on her lips.

Craig waited until Brian and Kyle were done then grabbed a cup for himself. He watched Jasmine's growing anxiety as he poured the coffee and didn't notice the liquid approaching the top of the cup until it was too late. The hot coffee overflowed, burning his fingers and making him drop his cup with a yelp of pain. Brian, Jasmine, and Dr. Kurtsman all jumped up to help him but Kyle stayed seated, staring at the floor in front of him. Craig dabbed at his raw, red skin with a napkin, taking a cold bottle of water to press against the burn. He sat next to Kyle and asked what was going on with him but got no response.

Jasmine finished helping Dr. Kurtsman clean up. She got another cup of coffee and offered it to Craig but he shook his head. She set it down next to her previous cup then took her seat once more next to the empty sixth one. She watched as Brian shook Kyle, demanding to know what was going on but Kyle never lost his thousand yard stare. She wanted to interject but movement by the door caught her eye. She shifted for a better look. When she saw who was standing there, her entire face darkened.

Jasmine sat bolt upright, staring down the younger girl, protectively pulling the empty chair closer to her. Mandy stood playing with the strap of her purse, asking if she was in the right place for the PTSD support group. Dr. Kurtsman got up to welcome her but Jasmine rushed past him to confront her. At the sudden burst of movement, Kyle finally seemed to come back to the present. He jumped up and grabbed Jasmine before she could reach Mandy. Jasmine thrashed to get away but he held her tight. She started screaming that Mandy was just as bad as the rest of the horrible girls at her school and had no right to invade their meetings.

Dr. Kurtsman got to Mandy and escorted her past Jasmine who had started crying in Kyle's arms. He gave his seat to Mandy, not wanting to make things worse by giving her the seat he knew had been set up in honor of Rachel. Mandy did take the offered chair but she was shaking, eyes on Jasmine. Dr. Kurtsman announced he had invited her to the meeting. He told the group she had considered Rachel a good friend and was hurting over the loss. Jasmine snorted in derision at the comment but she stopped fighting against Kyle.

Mandy looked up around the small circle. She shook her head, mumbling it was a bad idea, that she shouldn't have come. She began getting to her feet but Dr. Kurtsman told her she was welcome in the group and he believed she should stay. He told everyone Mandy was hurting. She felt guilty about not doing more to help but she had been scared of ending up like Rachel, getting bullied constantly. He said they all knew how hard that was for Rachel and they should understand why Mandy chose as she did. She hung her head as he said the last part. Tears escaped her eyes that she swiped at quickly.

In a quiet voice she told the remaining members of the group how she saw Rachel struggle through each day. The way the others on the team called her names and tormented her. How Emily would tease her or spread lies to the rest of the school. Rachel would walk into a room and all conversation would stop. She had even heard a boy tried to assault her behind the school when she came to school to quit the team. She wanted desperately to tell everyone to stop but she knew she would just end up being another target and they would amp up what they were doing to Rachel as well. She didn't want to make things worse for herself or the girl she looked up to. She knew she was a coward but she honestly didn't thing she could do anything to help.

Jasmine's body relaxed and Kyle finally let her go. Slowly, she walked over to Mandy and held out a hand. Mandy stared up at her for a moment before taking it. Jasmine pulled her up into an embrace. The girls hugged for a long time but neither cried. They just held each other for strength. When they pulled apart Jasmine once again took on the happy deameaner she had before Mandy walked in. It was like a switch got flipped in her head. As soon as he sees Jasmine go back into her happy mode, Kyle falls back into his distant mood as well.

When everyone has taken their seats again, Dr. Kurtsman set up a seventh chair to keep the one next to Jasmine empty, she looked around and asked everyone how they were doing. Craig leaned forward, giving her a penetrating look and asked her how she was doing instead. Her eyes clouded over briefly but she waved a hand to dismiss the question before asking again how everyone is feeling this week.

Craig got up and knelt in front of her. "Are we really doing this?" He looked into her eyes. "Jasmine, Rachel killed herself. Now you are sitting here acting like a robot, Kyle is off in another dimension, and you want to ask how we are all doing. What the hell is going on with you?"

She blinked at him. "Craig, I appreciate your concern and clearly you are still in shock, I'm sure we all will be for awhile."

"Why are you acting like everything is ok? Like you didn't just practically attack Mandy when she came in? We all miss Rachel but I know you two were very close. Talk to us. We are a support group Jasmine, let us support you."

"Of course we all miss her." She smiled her infuriating smirk at him. "But I am choosing to remember her in my heart. In fact I got everyone a present. I did some research and found out yellow roses are the friendship flower." She got up and retrieved a small bag from the kitchenette. She pulled out a yellow rose and handed one to each of them except Mandy. "I'm sorry, I don't have enough because I didn't know you would be here. I will bring one for you next week I promise."

Mandy gave her a wide-eyed stare while Dr. Kurtsman leaned in, trying to make eye contact with Jasmine. "Jasmine? What you're doing isn't healthy. You're burying your feelings and that will eventually make you explode inside."

"I'm not burying anything." She insisted, taking her seat again.

"You can't even say her name. We have all said it but you flinch whenever someone says Rachel's name. You sit there and ask everyone how they are feeling but refuse to answer the question honestly yourself. You are hurting and that makes sense. You need to talk to us, Jasmine."

"I did answer the question, I'm fine. Look at me, I am doing better than ever." She gave them the frozen smile one last time.

Kyle leapt to his feet so fast the chair tumbled backward. "Fine? You think you're fine? Do us a favor and stop treating us like we're idiots, ok? You are the least fine of any of us."

She sat up straighter, smile faltering for a moment but stayed silent as he began to pace. Everyone in the group shrank back from him, trying not to catch his eye but he seemed completely focused on Jasmine. Finally she spoke. "Kyle, sit down so we can have our meeting, you're being rude. We need to give people who need it time to share."

"You're unbelievable, you know that? But hey, you mentioned sharing, go ahead." He gestured for her to speak.

"I don't have anything to share." She watched him carefully.
"We come here to share our feelings and I told you all I feel fine so I am done. Moving on."

"You have everything to share!" He exploded in frustration.
"No one here knows anything about you other than you blame yourself for a relationship that ended poorly. You are so secretive that no one here can say what brought you to us or to therapy in the

first place. Maybe nothing is wrong with you. Maybe you just like being a part of groups because you like attention. Maybe nothing happened to you at all."

Jasmine stood up, staring him down. He stopped pacing and faced her from across the circle. The standoff felt like it lasted for an eternity before she gritted her teeth and told him to sit down. She said she had nothing to share and that was what she meant. She turned her back on him and he reached out and grabbed her again. He hugged her to his chest, demanding to know what happened to her. He said if they really were the family Rachel claimed they were, than they had a right to know.

She slipped out of his grasp, panting, with tears sparkling in the corners of her eyes. Her glare was ice cold. "Fine, you want to know my story? Read it for yourselves."

She unzipped the hoodie she always wore, letting it drop to the floor. Underneath she was skin and bones. The sucking in of breath told her they had never suspected what she actually looked like. Her jeans were baggy to hide the same situation but they hung on her hips. Her tank top clung to her skinny frame now visible. She was covered in scars. Deep, angry slashes cut into her arms, shoulders and the top of her chest. Everyone's eyes widened and their jaws hung open as she lifted the bottom of her shirt to reveal more cuts across her torso. She does a full turn so they can see the marks go all the way around. She told them all if they wanted to read her story they could in the marks the knife left behind.

Brian regained his composure first. "Ok, so clearly you're a cutter, why should we care about that?"

"What?" Jasmine asked, confused by the question.

"You said you were in a bad relationship. We can all see what you did. Obviously the guy ignored you and you cut yourself for attention."

She was stunned speechless. She looked around the circle at everyone in turn. She started with Brian and ended with Kyle who was back to looking at the ground. "Don't you dare look away from me. You wanted to know and now you can see, this is what you were so eager to know. I loved my ex. I would have done anything for him and I tried. I made sure I looked perfect, acted perfect, everything about me had to be perfect all day, everyday. No matter how many times he told me I was ugly, stupid, or a waste of his time, I kept trying to be perfect for him. I spent years being the best I could be for him and when he decided he was bored with me and wanted to break up, he did it with a six-inch switchblade knife. His idea of a break up was more of a permanent one."

Dr. Kurtsman looked up at her. He could see the pain in her eyes as she told her story but there was something else there as well, shame. She was embarrassed. "Jasmine, it wasn't your fault."

"I felt like it was. I blamed myself for making him resort to that kind of reaction. I wasn't good enough and he was just doing what he had to to fix the situation." Tears poured down her face. Breathing hard she slowly sank to the ground in the middle of the circle of chairs. Mandy moved down onto the floor with her and took her hand. Eventually everyone moved down to sit around her. When she had her emotions back under control she gave a weak smile to Mandy, squeezing her hand. She agreed to share anything else they wanted to know because she knew Rachel would have wanted her to share her story.

Brian looked relieved and leaned over to whisper to Kyle they could finally wrap up the meeting and go back to fix his car. Kyle gave him a dull look but didn't say anything. Dr. Kurtsman watched the exchange then turned back to Jasmine. Kyle looked back at

Jasmine and to Dr. Kurtsman's amazement, seemed to be studying her. Without the hoodie Jasmine was smaller and more vulnerable looking than she had appeared at first in the meetings. She was also very pretty despite the numerous scars. Kyle appeared to have noticed that too.

Craig on the other hand was watching her like a father watches a daughter he is worried about. Dr. Kurtsman believed he had felt the same way about Rachel and was transferring those feelings to the other girl now that she also appeared to be in trouble. Brian was looking out the door, ignoring the situation while Mandy sat between him and Jasmine, listening intently.

"Why didn't your parents help you?" Kyle asked.

"They would have if they had known but I didn't confide in them about any of it. They would have made us break up."

"That seems like it would have been a good thing, considering." Brian said.

She glanced at him out of the corner of her eye. "I know that now but it was different then. He had me convinced my parents would see me as a disappointment and embarrassment, not the victim I was. I had to be perfect everyday so admitting something was wrong was out of the question because it would mean I wasn't."

No one seemed to know how to respond to that. She told them the highlights of their last fight from the argument that started it and the injuries she suffered, ending with how she escaped up the basement stairs only after she managed to kick the knife out of his hands. She told them there was a point she didn't plan to run away to which Brian replied she must have been stupid. Kyle told him to shut up then asked Jasmine to go on.

She said she knew she was broken but she used to be a lot worse. Dr. Kurtsman asked her what happened to her ex. She admitted that nothing happened at first. She was embarrassed and he had a friend that claimed he saw them get mugged. She didn't correct the story at first after awhile she came forward with the truth and told the police. She rubbed at her left wrist where a nasty scar could be seen without her hoodie. She got up and walked unsteadily to the counter to refresh her coffee. However when she got there she dropped the cup as her body began to shake all over. To everyone's horror, Jasmine's body gave out and she crumpled to the floor.

# Chapter 13

Brian stood watching the scene play out in slow motion. As Jasmine fell to the ground the world seemed to stand still, holding its breath. The second her body connected with the ground, everything changed. Craig jumped up, reaching for his phone to call an ambulance. Dr. Kurtsman also was up, sliding down next to where she lay, trying to revive her. Mandy and Kyle stayed where they were but Mandy's mouth hung open in shock, her eyes wide as she watched everything unfold. Kyle was the only one who was indifferent.

He sat like a statue on the ground near where Jasmine had been crying. The detachment written plainly on his face. Brian smirked. It was about time his friend saw how pointless this all was. He had been worried there was something developing between Kyle and Jasmine, some deeper feelings trying to take hold, but he could see from the look on Kyle's face if anything was there it was all on her side.

It was a relief to see that sob story she told didn't get to him. Brian had seen through the attention grabbing desperation to the pathetic truth. She was a drama queen and a crybaby. Looking at her it was obvious why the guy hadn't wanted to keep her around. He didn't believe for a second the scars weren't all self harm. She clearly liked being seen and what better way to cause sympathy than the shock and awe of the scars? Brian shook his head as he turned away. He walked over to get some more coffee and another donut, muttering to himself about needing to get away from the crazies.

While he was busy, the ambulance pulled up to get Jasmine. Lost in thought, Brian didn't hear all the chaos behind him as she was loaded up. He stayed focused on his coffee and snacks. He was also thinking about getting his car running again. It was the strangest thing. He had been working on cars with his father most of his life but for some reason his current one wouldn't work properly and no matter what he did, he couldn't seem to fix it. He mentally ran through all of the parts he had already examined and either repaired of replaced. None of them had worked. He bought more new parts he would be putting in as soon as Kyle got there after the meeting.

Someone shook him from his thoughts. Kyle must be ready to go. Brian turned to see Craig looking at him. "You ok, man?"

Brian snapped back to the present. He looked around the room and saw all of the chairs had been put away. The posters were down off the wall too. He turned back to look at the kitchen. Everything was gone. How had he been staring in that direction and somehow missed things being put away right in front of him? Craig was still staring at him, concern in his eyes. That was when he realized they were alone in the room. Dr Kurtsman, Mandy, even Kyle, all gone.

"Where is everyone?" He asked, still looking around as though they were hiding from him.

"Mandy left. She is really shaken up. I hope she comes back but after the outburst then seeing Jasmine rushed to the hospital I'm not sure she ever will." Craig looked back toward the door as though following the path she took as she exited. "Dr. Kurtsman followed behind the ambulance. Kyle tried to get in with her but they told him it was only for family or professionals so he took off after the doc. I have a stop to make but will go check in on her later. What about you?"

"Why did Kyle go? There was nothing wrong with him." Brian stared back at Craig.

"He said he wanted to go help in case she needed anything. I think he felt guilty for yelling at her; like her panic attack was his fault somehow. It isn't of course, but that seemed to be the way he was thinking. He also found her phone and called her mom to meet them there so he went to meet up with her in case she had any questions."

"Seriously? Good God, he was supposed to help me with my car. I am getting sick and tired of being blown off for no good reason. That girl is a sinking ship dragging all of us down with her baggage."

Craig stands straighter, planting his feet, and facing Brian directly.
"Look Brian, clearly you don't care about her or anyone in this group except yourself. But the rest of us care about each other. Kyle obviously cares about Jasmine, everyone can see that."

"So he falls for the Titanic and leaves his brother high and dry? Got it, he's forgotten who and what is supposed to be important in his life. What the hell ever happened to loyalty?" Brian set his cup aside, shoving the last of his donut into his mouth. He stared out the door.

"He tried to tell you he was taking off. You were so wrapped up in yourself you never heard him. The ambulance had already left and he wanted to get there to help her mom. He was the one acting like he had priorities that made sense, you're just selfish." Craig said.

Brian turned back to him, rage flashing in his eyes, hands balling into fists. He took a few steps toward Craig making the other man back up. Just as Brian was preparing to take his frustrations out on Craig, his phone rang in his pocket. He pulled it out and saw Kyle's name on the screen. A smug look replaced the anger as he answered.
"Hey man, you want me to order pizza or should I pick up some burgers for us on the way to my place?"

"Go ahead and get whatever you want. I will pick up food on my way but don't wait for me. Her mom still hasn't gotten here and I need to make sure she is up to sped and Jasmine is ok before I take off. I will see you in awhile." Kyle didn't wait for a response before hanging up.

Brian's teeth clenched as he put the phone back in his pocket. He looked up to see Craig waiting by the door on the far side of the building. The rage was back in Brian but it was all focused on Kyle and Jasmine now. He walked stiffly down to the exit, passing Craig without a word or a glance. He heard Craig sigh in relief then lock the doors behind them. He called a cab and waited, seething at the thought of his brother in arms abandoning him in his time of need.

Craig walked out to his car. He had another meeting to go to but all Brain saw was a man running away. Craig looked back at the young man standing on the sidewalk waiting for a taxi to take him home. He thought about Dr. Kurtsman telling Kyle he thought the three of them should sit down to discuss their dynamic and try to get things under control. It sounded like a good and much needed idea to Craig at the moment. He was afraid Brian was getting dangerously close to snapping and hurting someone.

# Chapter 14

The hospital was chaos. Doctors and nurses flowed in and out around them, tests were ordered, everyone talking at once. Kyle was asked by three people almost simultaneously who he was and why he was standing there. When it was determined he wasn't family he was sent to the waiting area until she could be put into a room. She had regained consciousness during the ride but her anxiety was still sky high and threatened to pull her back under. When he left the room she was crying but he couldn't tell if he caused it or it was because he was leaving.

He sat in one of the uncomfortable chairs in the lobby. He had no idea what to do so he stared at the floor and cursed himself for causing her pain. He just wanted them all to heal and help each other but it seemed he was ruining things left and right. Jasmine was struggling with a panic attack he caused by pushing her and Brian would be pissed he wasn't on his way to help with the car. At the moment though, he was right where he believed he should be.

While he sat there, a woman approached him. "Excuse me young man, are you by chance Kyle Masters?"

He looked up. "Yes ma'am."

She held out a hand which he shook automatically, standing to greet her. "My name is Georgia Byers, I'm Jasmine's mom. We spoke on the phone."

"Yes ma'am." He said again. He waved an arm at the chair next to where he had been.

When they were both seated she looked at him appraisingly. "Thank you for calling. I have heard so many wonderful things about you and the support group. I think you are really helping her."

Kyle looked around the waiting area doubtfully. "I would have to respectfully disagree. Helping wouldn't generally involve a trip to the hospital."

Georgia smiled warmly. "You don't think so huh? Well I'm not surprised at all. Jasmine has a tendency to keep things internalized when they are really important to her then they all come streaming out at once. It is hard for her to share how she feels about herself but she will be the first warrior to stand up for another. I had a feeling after losing Rachel that this meeting would be tough for her, for all of you really."

"It was. But one of the most difficult parts was that she put out six chairs as though Rachel were still going to be there. She also put up posters of words Rachel came up with and we all made together last week. Seeing that stuff made it hard for the rest of us but I guess it was her way of coping with the loss."

Georgia frowned. "No, that sounds like denial, not acceptance and coping. Jasmine has struggled to make deep connections with people for years because she didn't believe there was anything more than skin deep worth liking about her. She is a pretty girl, she has been told that for most of her life, but she can't see it. Her real beauty is on the inside but she is so afraid to let anyone in that most people think she is stuck up and don't bother probing to get to know her which just reinforces her beliefs."

"I think she is special. I would love it if she would let me and the rest of the group get to know her better." Kyle said. He looked down, color rising in his cheeks. "The way she stepped up and protected Rachel was amazing to see and anyone that can care for others that deeply and want to guard them is definitely someone worth knowing."

"Then what is it that seems to be bothering you? You care about her and she is going to be fine, just remember what I said about her struggles and don't get discouraged, she will open up eventually." Georgia patted him on the shoulder.

"I just feel terrible because I'm the reason she is here. I caused the anxiety attack. I pushed her, not physically, but emotionally. She kept saying she was fine and it was clear she wasn't. I demanded she tell us what was going on but I had no idea what that would cause. She unzipped her hoodie and showed us the worst scars I have ever seen, and I've been to war. She is covered with them. She started screaming at us that we could read her story written across her body in them. I wanted to cry and throw up just looking at them. I can't imagine what she went through to get them."

The physical scars are bad." Georgia agrees. "The mental and emotional ones are worse. She was in a relationship with a boy who controlled her. He made my beautiful daughter think she was ugly and worthless. Worst of all, he made her believe she couldn't come to us and tell us what was happening. He was very good at what he did and she lives with the sound of his voice in her head telling her everyday that she is still nothing at all. That no one will care about her and she is incapable of love. You didn't cause this. You just made her face that voice and today it won."

"I never knew she was battling so much." Kyle said, staring off into the distance.

'She is waging war but she is stronger than she thinks. And so are the rest of you, for that matter. As long as you are willing to support and be supported, be honest and open up about your struggles, you are all capable of healing." Georgia shifts in her chair so she can look at him but also see the hallway where the doctors and nurses are coming through the doors. "Jasmine still blames herself for what happened. She is wrong but until she sees that for herself it will be an ongoing fight. I would personally like to wring Tyler's throat but that wouldn't help her. It would just put me in jail. I have to allow her to process it at her own speed."

"Do you know more about what happened to her? She told us there was a big fight and he hurt her. He used a knife to cut her and stab her because he wanted a permanent break up. She didn't give many details though."

"I wish I had known what was going on at the time. It is amazing how secretive teenagers can be. She kept us at arms length because of him and his manipulation but I still wish I could have seen it coming. He did try to kill her. He fractured her jaw, broke ribs, and you saw some of the scars. There are more, trust me. But even after that, he sent flowers to the hospital when she got away from him and she tried to apologize for causing the fight. It took so long for her to trust anyone enough to be honest and put that bastard behind bars where he belonged in the first place."

"She said a friend of his gave a report of them being mugged or jumped or something."

Georgia nodded. "The police came in to tell her not to be afraid, they would catch the person or people that attacked her and her boyfriend. She told them they hadn't been attacked at all. She said they had a fight because she wasn't good enough and he was doing the world a favor by getting rid of her. Once the truth was out and her statement had been taken I told my husband who would have killed her boyfriend with his bare hands if the police hadn't arrested him first. Jasmine had a few of these attacks leading up to it but she was brave and went to court, testified against him, and put him in jail where he belonged. He may be gone physically from her life but he damaged her so deeply it will take a long time to heal."

"She told us she is broken." Kyle told her.

"She isn't broken, she is fractured but healing. Like I said, you are all stronger than you know." Georgia sighed. "I know his voice talks to her in her mind constantly. It tells her the worst lies about herself. He almost took my baby away from me and while that voice nearly killed her it also saved her life once. I do my best to fight it by keeping my voice in there just as loud and making sure she knows she is loved and worthy each and every day. I hope you have a voice telling you how well you are doing too. You deserve to know it's true."

# Chapter 15

Brian got home, paid the driver, took his bag of remaining food and stomped into the house. His car was up on a lift in the garage, the engine in pieces waiting for him and Kyle to put it back together with the new parts but of course Kyle wasn't there. He was still taking care of that drama queen, Jasmine. It was such bullshit. He was done with the meetings, he decided. Kyle would have to make a choice. If they really were the brothers they had always claimed they were, he would be done with the meetings as well. It was a waste of time.

Kyle had been sucked in and brainwashed by the crybaby cult but he would rescue his friend, show him the true path to healing was all in his head, and Kyle would owe him for getting him out of there. Brian laughed to himself for the "crybaby cult" thought and headed out to the garage, stripping off his shirt as he went.

He opened the garage door for ventilation, and to let anyone passing by check him out with no shirt, then bent over the work table. He smiled to himself. He knew he looked good. He worked out constantly and was proud of his physique. The neighbors were welcome to ogle him, although not that many had recently he noticed. He walked around the garage, picking up pieces, examining them on the work table then getting another. He had started learning about cars by working on classics then progressed to helping his dad keep the family truck running for years. His father told him a real man could always count on his own two hands to keep going.

His current ride had a bad habit of stalling out while driving but no matter how much he worked on it he couldn't seem to pinpoint the problem. When he got done looking at the last of the remaining parts he wiped his hands on a rag then texted Kyle to ask where he was at before pulling out the new pieces. As he worked, he thought about the "support" group. He had agreed to go just to show Kyle what a stupid idea it was but somehow his buddy had fallen for their crap hook, line, and sinker. He knew it wasn't for them although he had expected to find people there with real problems. What he saw instead, though, was a handful of people whining about nothing.

Craig's accident killed his son and his wife left him. It sucked, sure, but it wasn't something to lose your mind over. He was sure Craig mourned his son, losing a four year old had to be rough. But people got divorced all the time and got over it. Rachel admitted she wasn't supposed to be at the party she went to when she claimed she had been raped. Even if it was true he believed she should have just taken it as a learning experience and moved on. Her suicide had been painful for some of the others but he knew he hadn't been affected by it. Besides it seemed more like she was just begging for attention. Slicing open her wrists, making a big mess, too flashy. If it was just about saying goodbye she could have taken a bunch of sleeping pills or done something else less bold.

Jasmine was by far the worst of the group. She acted superior to everyone else and defensive about her situation as well as about Rachel. She pretended to be a protector but then had a complete meltdown when forced to talk about her real situation, what a joke. Her problems were too important to share without a bunch of fanfare and now she was using her manipulative ways to sink her claws into Kyle, turning him against his real friends. And he was letting her do it.

Aggravation boiled over. He threw the wrench he had been using against the wall of the garage then stalked over to the refrigerator to get a beer. He drank deeply, leaning against the bench, telling his mind and body to relax. Every time he thought about her he could feel his body tense with rage. He squeezed the bottle but stopped just short of breaking the glass. A gentle breeze blew in from outside, helping cool his sweat covered torso. Finally he felt like he could concentrate on the car again. He walked back to the engine parts and cleaned them, reassembling as he worked. When he had it back together he ran a system flush on the fluids and topped them off before trying to start the car. It came to life and he smiled in victory. He fixed it and did it all himself. He didn't need anyone, not even Kyle. Which seemed like a good thing, since he was alone in the world after all.

Just then, the car stalled out again. He bellowed in rage, smashing the beer bottle. The glass cut his hand and the sounds scared a couple children riding by on their bikes. Brian didn't notice any of that, though. He kicked the bumper, glaring into the open engine compartment. Blood dripped down his hand, spattering on the concrete floor of the garage. All he could see was hours of work wasted. The parts were all new and he was positive they were put together perfectly. It could be something in the car's internal computer.

He swore under his breath as he considered being a mechanic was practically the same as working in an IT department these days. Everything was computerized. You practically needed a computer science degree to do anything. He wasn't afraid to get dirty but that didn't seem to be the way to fix the problem anymore. He slammed the hood, leaving a bloody handprint on top. He closed the garage door on his way back into the house. In the kitchen he grabbed two more beers in each hand then proceeded to the living room.

The time on his phone told him it was after nine. Kyle hadn't even had the decency to call or text that he was bailing on him tonight. He sat in front of the television, draining the first of the beers in three long swallows. He flipped through the channels, not really watching anything, and drinking his beers. He spent the next few hours that way, only getting up to relieve himself or replenish the supply of beer and grab some chips.

When he grabbed the last of the bottles he thought to himself he would have to make a beer run in the morning. It occurred in a distant part of his brain there had been a brand new twelve pack in the fridge when he started the night and it was now gone. But who cared? No one else bothered with him so why should he feel bad about enjoying his night?

After all the drinks were gone and the dead soldiers lined up along the edge of the coffee table, he got up to stumble off to bed. His bladder informed him they needed to make a detour to the bathroom first where he tripped over a towel on the floor and grabbed the counter to break his fall but all he managed to do was open the cut on his hand again. He paid it no mind, pissing and heading to the bedroom. He stripped off the rest of his clothes and collapsed in bed, falling asleep before his head hit the pillows. As soon as his eyes were closed, he was back in combat.

He saw himself running into the cafe. He heard and felt the blasts as both sides erupted into gunfire. His men fell around him. He screamed but no sound could be heard above the bullets ricocheting and flying by his head. He ran ahead to take charge but the other soldiers all retreated to an alley. He turned and made his way there but as soon as he reached them they dispersed without telling him the plan. Why were they acting like he was invisible?

He ran back out into the street not covered in dirt and blood. He tried to figure out how to get a handle on things because everyone else was just running scared but when he turned the corner he ran straight into Ammar who had somehow grown up and was holding an AK47 pointed directly at his chest. The rest of the soldiers were focused on the larger gun battle. They left him alone to die. Right then Ammar pulled the trigger and Brian woke up with a start.

He and his bed were soaked in a cold sweat. He was out of breath and disoriented. It took several minutes to feel normal again. The clock on the nightstand said it was half past eleven. He had been having a lot of those kinds of dreams lately though he wouldn't admit that to anyone because they would just try to make a big deal out of it. Even in the war memory dreams though, he had never been abandoned by his brothers before.

Brian tossed aside the damp covers and got up, pulling on a pair of camouflage shorts. He went out to the garage to retrieve his phone and wasn't surprised to see he had no missed calls or messages. He tried calling Kyle but got no answer. He tried again and the phone once more went straight to voicemail. Great, so now he was not only being abandoned in his dreams but in real life as well.

He walked back into the bedroom and tried to go back to sleep but as soon as he pulled the blanket over himself and felt the dampness he pushed it away again. The group claimed they were there for one another but here he was reaching out to his best friend and getting ignored. Where the hell was he? Brian got up and stalked back to the living room feeling lost and alone. He dropped into the recliner, leaning all the way back and staring up at the exposed beams in the ceiling. The vision popped into his mind instantly. He laughed as he pictured everyone finding him and knowing it was their fault. That their inconsiderate ways and lack of caring had pushed him over the edge.

He realized he could prove how dumb and pointless that group was with just one simple action. Showing it didn't help anyone heal it just isolated people. He went to the bedroom and pulled the sheet off the bed. Carrying it back out to the living room he tossed an end over the beam above his chair and secured it the way he had been taught in his training. He got a notepad and scribbled a quick message. *You did this. You say you support but you only abandon. Where were any of you when I needed someone?* He got on the arm of the recliner and wrapped the loose end around his neck. He looked around the room one last time and then, with a giant middle finger to the world, Brian Nickerson stepped off the chair.

# Chapter 16

Kyle spent time talking to Jasmine once she was in her room and he had gotten a lot of insight from her mom. They had gone to the cafeteria after visiting hours and she listened as he talked about his feelings over Rachel's suicide, Jasmine and her situation, the group in general, his own pain and his debate about whether to continue as a soldier, everything. It felt amazing to open up and share with someone unbiased and willing to not judge but simply listen.

At one point Georgia yawned and Kyle realized it must be getting late. He had lost all track of time in the basement cafeteria so when he looked at his phone he was startled to see it was after eleven. He noticed he had a few missed calls from Brian and he knew he was in trouble with his friend. He felt guilty for taking so long but if he knew his best friend, he would still be out working on the car and preparing to gloat about figuring it out all on his own. He tried to return the call but got no answer. That wasn't really surprising. Between him being mad at Kyle and probably on his back under the car, the call wouldn't be a priority at the moment.

As he left the hospital he debated driving home and just going to help in the morning but he didn't want to have more of a fight than he was already in for. As it was there would be groveling involved he was sure. He got a couple burgers on his way over and arrived just before midnight. The garage door was closed but Brian was just probably keeping the noise down so neighbors wouldn't complain. He wasn't always so courteous but sometimes he did that. Kyle went in through the front door, depositing the bag from his burgers in the trashcan in the kitchen. He called out he was sorry for taking so long and he knew he would have to make up for it but he was there and wanted to help. He asked how the car was coming along but got no answer.

He called out again but got nothing in response. He asked how long the silent treatment was going to last and waited, still Brian said nothing. Could he be asleep? Kyle thought to himself. It seemed early for Brian, especially when he was all wound up, but it was possible. He stopped in the middle of the kitchen, listening for snores. Instead he heard a creaking coming from the living room. He must be rocking in his recliner, enjoying the begging for forgiveness.

"Ok man, you win. I know you're pissed at me and you have every right to be but I was just trying to do the right thing and be there for Jasmine after I caused her to have the meltdown." Nothing. "Brian, what the hell? You planning to punish me forever?"

He walked into the dining room and down the hall leading toward the living room. The creaking sound grew louder. Halfway down the hall he stopped and leaned his back against the wall. "Dude, you have to forgive me. I know you think the group is stupid and maybe for you it is. But it is helping me and I wish you would just open up and share; you might find the support helpful as well. You aren't weak and being in the group doesn't make anyone think you are. We all need help sometimes and if you stop fighting it and take a good look inside I think you will see I'm right. Please talk to me so we can work things out before anything bad happens."

Nothing came from the living room but the creaking sound. Pushing himself away from the wall Kyle took a deep breath to control his frustrations. He walked around the corner into the living room. "Brian just give me a minute to..."

He trailed off when he saw his best friend hanging from the ceiling beam. His body swung gently, creating the creaking Kyle had mistaken for the recliner. He face was swollen and his tongue was hanging out. Worst of all, his bulging, bloodshot eyes were staring right at Kyle. A small yelp came out. Sliding down to the floor Kyle wanted to cry, to scream, to do anything but he simply knelt there, staring up at the face of the man who had been his brother since they were children.

He looked up at Brian's accusing eyes, bile rising in his throat. He forced it back down and climbed to his feet. He had to get Brian down. This was not a fitting and for a soldier. He ran to the kitchen all the while telling himself it was just a dream, a nightmare, not real. He pulled the butcher knife from a drawer, turned and ran back but his body stopped him at the end of the hall. He took a deep breath and forced himself to reenter the room. He stood in front of Brian and his body overruled him. He dropped to his knees, pulling the wastebasket Brian usually used for empty bottles closer, and threw up. He wretched until nothing was left. After he was sure he was done he shoved the trashcan away and climbed onto the recliner. He stood behind his friend's body where the eyes couldn't watch him as he cut the sheet.

He sawed at it but made no progress. He needed slack in the sheet but for once his training failed him. He couldn't touch his friend to lift his body. He tried but his arms refused to wrap themselves around his body and make the nightmare real. Sobbing, he got back down and pulled out his phone to call the police.

He reported the suicide to the dispatcher then went back to the kitchen where his stomach heaved again. When he was done he curled up on the floor and told the dispatcher he had come in through the front door using the spare key. He said the door was still unlocked. When the sirens wailed up in front of the house minutes later Kyle was still in the fetal position on the kitchen floor crying and dry heaving. However, when the first officers came into the house he forced himself to get up and show them where his friend still swung.

One of the officers stood beneath Brian, holding his feet to give the other office slack to cut him down. The man holding Brian lost his grip when the full amount of his weight dropped and the body fell to the floor with a sickening thud. It was the last sound Kyle heard before he passed out, landing on the ground next to his best friend.

## Chapter 17

Just after one in the morning, Jasmine awoke to the sound of a phone buzzing. She groped for the landline in her hospital room but when she lifted the phone to her ear she heard a dial tone. She still said hello a couple of times before her sleep deprived brain realized it was the wrong one. She put the phone back in the cradle and sat up, rubbing her eyes and trying to focus. After a moment she saw the dull light of her cell phone screen lighting up as it vibrated on the table next to the bed. The name told her Dr. Kurtsman was calling.

Panic gripped her heart as she snatched up the phone. "Hello? Dr. Kurtsman? What happened?"

The doctor's calm voice had been replaced by a hoarser version. He sounded exhausted and something else but she couldn't put her finger on it. "Jasmine, I'm afraid I have some bad news. I didn't want to bother you with this but I also didn't want you to hear it on the news instead of from one of us. Tonight Kyle..."

Jasmine's heart jumped into her throat. "Kyle? No, please not Kyle. Why would he do something to himself. Please tell me he is ok. Tell me Kyle isn't hurt or dead."

"No, Kyle isn't hurt, at least not physically. Tonight Kyle came over to Brian's to help him work on his car but when he got to the house he found Brian dead. He hung himself Jasmine. Brian is gone."

Jasmine felt a flood of relief followed by a larger one of guilt and shame. She didn't want anything to happen to the members of the group, even Brian. But she cared so much about Kyle and it felt like they were becoming friends. It broke her heart to think about something happening to him, but she chided herself, that doesn't mean she should have been relieved to find out it was another member instead. "I'm going to get ahold of my doctor and get out of here. I should be on my way to you soon."

"No Jasmine." His tone stopped her in her tracks. "Stay where you are. The police have control of the scene. There is nothing you can do here and you need to rest and get yourself taken care of."

"But I want to be there for everyone and make sure Kyle is ok." She could hear the pleading in her voice but didn't care. "He was there for me. I need to return the favor."

"Now is not the time. Stay put. I know you are supposed to get out in the morning, we can all meet up for breakfast at that time and I will hopefully have more information for you by then." He hung up before she could say anything else. She hated the idea of just sitting there, doing nothing. She leaned back into the pillows, knowing she wasn't going back to sleep. There were too many questions. What happened to Brian? Dr. Kurtsman hadn't said. How was Kyle doing after finding him? She couldn't imagine he was doing very well. What would happen to their group? It kept getting smaller. Would they even bother to keep going after this? She didn't know.

Kyle had to be going out of his mind, and after he had been with her and so supportive all day. He needed her to do the same right then. She reached for her phone and dialed Kyle's number. They had all exchanged them during the first meeting and she was thankful for that now. She listened as the phone rang twice but in the middle of the third ring it clicked over to voicemail. She tried again and this time it was sent to voicemail on the first ring. He must still be talking to the police, she thought. Dr. Kurtsman had mentioned they were there.

She sat staring at the wall in front of her, absently massaging the scar on her right wrist. Even if she acknowledged Mandy as a real member of the group she couldn't get past the fact the group was shrinking. Rachel died, now they lost another. The thought made her feel cold inside. She pulled the blanket, trying to get warm. She wanted to turn on her side, to curl up and cry, but the blanket was caught on something. She tugged hard. It had been caught on her IV line and when she tugged it nearly pulled the needle out of her arm. She yelped in pain, tears coming quickly.

She cast away the blanket and held the now throbbing arm close to her body. She quietly scolded herself, asking how she could be so stupid to do something like that. Her fingertips probed the now awkward angle of the IV needle. She could hear the hysterical laughter from the voice of her ex boyfriend echoing in her head. It told her she would be the story the nurses shared about dumb patients. It also said Kyle didn't care about her, he just pitied her. The voice told her she is alone and that is all she deserved. Her knees slid up and she hugged them as she began to cry. The blanket slipped down again, revealing even more scars.

When she curled her legs up she accidentally hit the call button and a nearby nurse came to see what she needed. When she got to the doorway she stopped dead in her tracks. She knew the girl in the bed had been brought in for a severe anxiety attack. She was there under observation but at the moment she looked like she had given up, like a broken doll thrown aside. She approached slowly, trying not to startle the poor girl. She called out Jasmine's name but got no acknowledgment. She tried again and still nothing. When she reached out to tap her on the shoulder, the reaction was instant and violent. Jasmine flailed, yanking the IV line the rest of the way out as she flailed around. The nurse backed up against the far wall. She watched with mounting horror as blood gushed from the hole created by the extracted needle.

She radioed for the doctor who joined her moments later. Together the restrained Jasmine and got a new IV line in her then gave her a sedative. The medicine took effect quickly and she stopped fighting them. When she was lying still again they cleaned her up and bandaged the wound in her arm.

Through glassy eyes, Jasmine watched them leave, the doctor stopping in the doorway to look at her the way the nurse had done when she entered. He decided to contact the psychology department and see if she had a therapist of record. If she didn't he would have someone from the hospital take a look at her. The scars he saw were bad, but she clearly had wounds inside and out that needed to be addressed.

# Chapter 18

Craig watched Kyle as he sat on the curb in front of Brian's house. When Dr. Kurtsman called he had said there was no reason for him to go but by the end of the call Craig was already out of bed, dressed, and in the car. He got the address after informing the doc he was coming no matter what and would simply drive around until he found it if necessary. Once he had the address it only took a few minutes to get to the house.

Kyle had been in the same spot he currently occupied when he arrived. He wasn't crying, just sitting there. He stared at the ground in front of him. Craig leaned against the front of the house, next to the door, watching the first responders as they came and went. Dr. Kurtsman sat on the edge of the porch doing the same. Kyle was in the middle of the chaos but sat like a statue, unaware of his surroundings. Craig walked over, clapped Dr. Kurtsman on the shoulder, then made his way out to sit with Kyle. As he dropped onto the curb he couldn't help but think about Brian; about his motivations.

How could a man who claimed to be so independent, to not need anyone and constantly insisted he was perfectly ok turn to something so desperate? The look on Kyle's face told him he was thinking the same thing. In truth, Craig had always believed Brian probably needed more help than any of them. He was angry and aggressive to hide that he was scared of being vulnerable. He attacked others feelings to hide his own and laughed off everything to keep from showing he cared or wanted to be cared about. Even the note he had written blaming everyone else for his suicide seemed like him taking yet another opportunity to hide from the truth.

Craig wanted to shrug it all off. He and Brian hadn't been close. Hell, they hadn't really liked each other at all. But with the recent loss of Rachel and now another hit to their tiny family, he was feeling it more than he had expected. He wondered again what the rest of them could have done to show Rachel and Brian the group was a safe place. He hoped Mandy wouldn't give up because of all this.

Next to him, Kyle was speaking quietly to himself. Craig listened but it took a few minutes to be sure of what he was hearing. Kyle was repeating the Army Oath over and over. "I, Kyle Masters, do solemnly swear that I will support and defend the Constitution of the United States against all enemies, foreign and domestic; that I will bear true faith and allegiance to the same; and that I will obey the order of the President of the United States and the orders of offices appointed over me, according to regulations and the Uniform Code of Military Justice. So help me God."

Craig realized how few times he had heard Kyle's last name and that he had heard Brian's even less. He was sitting with a man he barely knew, mourning the loss of another he knew less. Yet he felt closer to either than most people in his life because of the experiences they shared. Even though Kyle had never lost a son and Craig would never go to war, they were both survivors of horrible situations and that created a bond. Dr. Kurtsman had talked about that when he said to switch their thinking and stop being victims, instead be survivors. He told them all to do that. Which meant he thought of them all on the same playing field. It was a strange realization to contemplate where he was but it was there nevertheless.

It wasn't until they went to the church that he learned Rachel's last name was Morris and he had learned that seeing it in a program for her funeral. Jasmine was sitting in the hospital right now and he had no idea what her last name was. At the same time he felt bonded to them, he also felt completely disconnected.

He stood and stretched, seeing the foot traffic in and out of the house slowing down. Kyle didn't seem to notice any of it. Craig opened his mouth to say something, anything, to Kyle but nothing came out. He hung his head and trudged back up the lawn to sit and wait for everything to wrap up. Dr. Kurtsman looked up at him when he came back and sat down next to him on the step. "I can't imagine what Kyle is going through. Being a foster kid who was practically adopted by the Nickerson family, this must make him feel like he is completely alone. I know Brian's father passed away and his mother was never in the picture. He has a younger brother but I don't know the name. I'm sure Kyle does though."

Craig watched Kyle. The police had attempted to question him earlier after they informed him he couldn't go to the morgue with Brian's body. Dr. Kurtsman had stepped in to answer as much as possible in order to keep people from overwhelming Kyle and had asked the paramedics to take a look at him for possible signs of shock. They recommended he go to the hospital but he had refused so far. Dr. Kurtsman asked them to wait, knowing it was the right place for Kyle to be but he would have to process that and make the decision himself.

"I wish I knew what to say or do to help him." Craig murmured.

"I understand. It's hard sitting on the sidelines and not being able to do anything but watch. I can talk all day about statistics and the clinical side of these kind of things but when you're experiencing deep pain logic will never trump emotion. Right now nothing we say will make a bit of difference."

Craig nodded. He noticed one of the paramedics looking over at him a few times but didn't know why. He ran through names and faces in his mind and the guy looked sort of familiar but he couldn't be sure. His attention was torn away when Kyle finally moved. He pulled his legs in, resting his folded arms on his knees and looking like the lonely little boy he must have been once. The paramedics began loading their equipment and Dr. Kurtsman made his way down to tell Kyle he thought it would be best if he went with them to the hospital. He tells the young soldier he can be given something to help him sleep and then they can all talk more in the morning.

   Kyle looked up at him with glassy eyes but nodded numbly and let himself be led to the waiting ambulance. Dr. Kurtsman wobbled on his feet as he helped Kyle get in the back and Craig rushed up behind to keep the older man from falling. Dr. Kurtsman gave him a grateful, tired smile then reached in and squeezed Kyle's hand. He told the paramedics to take care of him as they closed the doors. Craig asked if he was doing ok and he nodded saying he was just exhausted and it had been a very long week for everyone.

# Chapter 19

When the sun rose the next morning, sending golden slants of light through the blinds in her room, Jasmine was already wide awake. After hearing the news about Brian she had barely slept. Instead she spent the hours before dawn thinking about losing Rachel and all the things she wished she could have done to save her. She only considered taking her own life once and was happy she hadn't gone through with it but she did understand the feeling of desperation. Jasmine's trauma had built over time. She faced days that turned into months that became years of being told she wasn't good enough, smart enough, worth loving. She remembered the feeling of wanting to die to escape it.

Rachel's incident happened quickly but was then perpetuated by those that bullied her and blamed her for the worst moment of her life. They made her relive it every moment of everyday and Jasmine could see where that would feel like there was no way out. She had another year of high school left and the prospect of facing those same people, of losing everything you had once held dear, must have seemed impossible. And her parents were the worst part of it in Jasmine's opinion. They deserved the majority of the blame for what happened. Not only did Rachel face her peers but she found no comfort or even love at home after enduring the trauma and frustrations of school life.

The thought of Rachel's parents made Jasmine's blood boil. They abandoned her at the funeral and the way everyone else treated her made her feel violated over and over again. The poor girl had confided the only time she felt safe and remotely understood was in group. It was the only place she felt like she could be herself and not be ashamed.

Jasmine remembered sitting at the park with her on that bench overlooking downtown. She had wanted so much to reach out and help Rachel but she didn't know how and now she was struggling because she missed her chance to do something when it could have made a difference. That thought brought up one of Mandy. The girl had said she wanted to help but was afraid. Jasmine had been so wrapped up in her own pain that she lashed out, not realizing she was just as guilty of not acting. Right then she knew Mandy was hurting just as bad as the rest of them. Jasmine had been wrong. She needed to fix it by bringing her into the circle and helping her the way she had failed to help Rachel. Mandy was part of the group now.

The group. They were down a member again. Brian was gone and she was completely baffled as to why. He had always been so insistent that he was fine on his own, that he didn't need any of them. In truth, Jasmine had been afraid of Brian. His temper and unpredictability had felt like the second coming of Tyler while his constant nagging to get Kyle out of the group could have resulted in two members leaving which would have destroyed a group she desperately needed.

She couldn't explain why but his suicide made her angry. Rachel's had seemed like an act of desperation and despair, Brian's on the other hand pissed her off for being selfish. She didn't know about the note blaming everyone else, but she always considered him a walking time bomb, waiting to take down the entire group. Now that he had gone off he had devastated his best friend and could possibly have succeeded in destroying the thing he hated most.

She wanted to be there for Kyle. It was a parallel situation. He lost Brian and she lost Rachel. Yes he had known Brian longer so there was more history between them but loss was loss and she knew she could be a support for him the way he had done for her after her meltdown the day before.

She looked around her room. It was a private room but instead of making her feel secure it made her feel isolated. Panic began to rise inside her again. She needed to get out of there and go be with the members of her group, her family. She wanted to apologize to Mandy and find Kyle to tell him she understood exactly what he was going through. Dr. Kurtsman had told her they would all go to breakfast but it was way too early for that. She needed out now so she could be with her people.

She carefully unhooked the wires from her body and located her clothes in the drawer of the table next to the bed. As quietly as possible she slid off the bed and put on her jeans. Her shirt was halfway on when she heard a voice talking behind her. She whirled around to see who it was and pulled on the IV line again. Her surprise was stronger than the pain that time and she managed to keep her reaction to a peep. The line stayed in place although her bruised skin gave a warning tingle of pain.

Craig stared at her from the doorway. "What exactly do you think you're doing?"

She was about to answer when her eyes locked on the steaming cups in his hand. His fatherly tone made her face flush like a kid caught with her hand in the cookie jar. She finished pulling her shirt down then sat back on the edge of the bed, accepting the cup he held out to her. She blew on it while watching him. He was standing in the room but positioned perfectly to block any escape attempt. She silently wondered if he knew all along she was a flight risk. "Why are you here so early? You didn't have to come visit me."

"You need to get back in bed until the doctors say you can leave." He gestured for her to lay back and put the wires back in place. "Dr. Kurtsman is here too and he won't be happy to see you trying to run away."

"I wasn't running away. I just needed to get out of here and go be with the group. We are supposed to have breakfast this morning, aren't we?" His expression told her he wasn't buying it. He stood his ground until she scooted back on the bed and pulled the blanket back up to her waist. He stepped aside but remained between her and the door.

She could see the exhaustion etched on his face. The bags under his eyes could have been packed for a long weekend and the crows feet at the corners of his eyes were deep. He sniffed his coffee, absorbing every ounce of energy he could before taking a sip. When Dr. Kurtsman came in she immediately asked how Kyle was doing. At first he gave no reply. He was leaning heavily on his cane and it took several minutes and breaks for him to walk across the room, even with Craig's help, to the chair next to her bed.

"Kyle is being treated for stress, shock, and exhaustion. He is struggling and we need to keep him in our thoughts and prayers." Before he could say more he started coughing hard. When he got it back under control he was out of breath. Jasmine wanted to ask what was wrong but looking at Craig's face again, she was sure Kyle wasn't the only one exhausted. Dr. Kurtsman had obviously been out all night and was paying for that now.

"Where is Kyle being treated? This is the only hospital I know of in Clydesburg." Craig and Dr. Kurtsman exchanged a glance. Neither answered her. "Come on, why won't you tell me? Is he here? I should go talk to him and see if there is anything I can do to help."

"Jasmine, Kyle is in a very vulnerable state right now. He needs to process what happened. I think it is best if we push breakfast back to dinner to make sure you are cleared to leave and he is ready to be around people again. I already spoke with Mandy and Craig. We all agree it is best to wait."

She crossed her arms over her chest, being careful to not pull on her IV. "Where is he, Dr. Kurtsman? He was there for me yesterday and I need to be there for him now."

Dr. Kurtsman struggled to his feet. The simple action once again made him wheeze for breath. When he could manage, he headed for the door with Craig following right behind. Craig stayed close, looking out the door so he could avoid her gaze. She begged for an answer but neither answered her. When they reach the hallway a nurse stopped them. She overheard the nurse's chipper response to a question Dr. Kurtsman had asked. "Yes doctor, he is in room five seventeen. He is still heavily sedated but you are welcome to check in on him."

Jasmine had suspected he was in the same hospital but why would they hide it from her? Why was she being shut out? Did they think she was too fragile? Were they treating her with kid gloves because of her panic attack? She needed to figure out how to get back in the loop before she was removed forever.

She got released a few hours later. Dr. Kurtsman and Craig never came back to check in on her but she had gotten a text that dinner was being postponed and she would hear from them when it was rescheduled. Her mother came to take her home but she said she needed to visit a friend in another room and would call when she needed a ride. Georgia hesitated but agreed to come back after she went to run a couple of errands. She signed her discharge paperwork and got dressed before following the nurse down the hall. The lobby button was already pushed but just before the doors slid closed completely, Jasmine pushed five. When they opened again she made her way down the hall to five seventeen to see Kyle.

She walked slowly, listening for either Dr. Kurtsman's or Craig's voices but neither could be heard. She paused at the doorway the way people kept doing to her. She slipped into the room where his steady breathing came from the far side of the curtain. Kyle was asleep. Obviously the information she overheard about him being sedated was still true. She sat down in the chair next to his bed.

Reaching out to hold his hand, she laid her head next to it and began to cry.

# Chapter 20

Kyle woke up when he felt someone holding his hand. He looked over through the haze of the drugs they had given him and saw Jasmine crying next to him. He immediately pulled his hand away from her. She looked up and reached for him again but he sat up and slid to the far side of the bed away from her. Confusion blossomed in her eyes.

"What's wrong?" She asked, wiping away her tears. "It's me."

"I can see who it is." His eyes narrowed as he looked at her. "What the hell do you want?"

The words hit her like a slap in the face as he spat them out. She opened her mouth to reply but he glared at her with dead eyes and she closed it again without saying anything. She shook her head to answer him instead. She didn't know what to say. He could see her trying to hold back tears but he found he didn't care one way or the other if she cried. The warmth he had felt for her the day before was now nothing more than ice in his veins. She locked eyes with him for a moment and he heard her whisper. "I just wanted to let you know I was here."

"I know you're here, that's the problem. You were here yesterday too and I was here with you. Now because I wasted my time playing around with you my best friend is dead." The dead stare continued.

The statement made the tears on her face freeze. She got to her feet, shaking. Her hands balled into fists at her sides but her words were calm. "You really think it's my fault he killed himself?"

If I hadn't been here tending to you and your stupid problems I would have been with him where I should have been. If I was there he never would have felt abandoned and done it. He killed himself because no one was there and I should have been but I was stuck here with you while you threw your pathetic little temper tantrum."

She stepped forward, looking him in the eye. "That is bullshit and you know it. He needed help and the entire group tried to give it to him just to have it thrown back in their faces. What he did was on him and deep down you know I'm right."

"How dare you talk about him like you ever gave a damn about him. Brian wasn't your best friend, your brother, You have no idea what it is like to go through war. We survived together and now it is just me left. I am alone because he is never coming back and you will never understand the pain and frustration of that." He insisted.

"Are you kidding me?" She took off her jacket, revealing her scars again. "I don't know about fighting to survive? I don't understand pain and suffering? I have never experienced loss? What about Rachel? Have you forgotten about her?"

"Oh, of course not. How could anyone ever forget about poor innocent little Rachel? Even if we wanted to you will never let us. She died. She killed herself like Brian did. The sad part is you only see one of them, the one you cared about."

"I cared about Brian!" She shouted at him. "He was a hothead, a pain in the ass, but it was obvious he was that way as a defense mechanism. He was in more pain than the rest of us, how can you not see that?" She pleaded with him.

"Now I can. He needed me, needed his brother but I was here, with you." He could see the rage building in her eyes and inwardly he smiled. He was glad he was pissing her off. You distracted me and now I am alone."

"You are not alone, the group is here for you." She tried to take his hand once more but was rejected.

"Group? What group? You people can go play together, pretending you're doing something worthwhile but there is nothing there for me and there wasn't anything for Brian either. He was right, it was a waste of time and so are you. Get out."

"I'm not leaving." She stood her ground. "You're upset and that's understandable but you shouldn't be alone."

"You don't get it, do you?" He glared at her.

"No, I don't understand why you're acting this way. I care about you and just want to help." She approached the side of the bed again.

He sat up straight, looking her in the eye. His voice was calm and steady when he addressed her. "Can you not hear me Jasmine? I said get out, bitch. You are nothing. You have always been nothing and that is how you are going to stay. There is no group. It's over. I never want to see you again. Get out!"

He screamed the last part, grabbing for the first thing he could get his hand on which was the landline phone. He threw it at her with all of his strength. It flew through the air but the cord caught and kept it from making it all the way to her. He saw his words cut through her like a knife as she began to cry, turning and running from the room.

# Chapter 21

Craig stood in the hallway next to Dr. Kurtsman as Jasmine ran by, tears streaming down her face. As she pushed her way into the stairwell at the end of the hall he turned to follow her but the Dr. Kurtsman put a hand on his arm to stop him. Craig looked back over his shoulder, confused.

"Let her go, Craig." He said. "She needs to have some time to deal with her emotions right now."

"Are you sure? She looked really upset. I sort of thought she might need a friend or at least a listening ear." Craig stared at the door she had disappeared through.

"I told her not to go visit with him but she didn't listen to me. I knew a confrontation was coming and I did my best to warn her. Now she has to process how it all went down. He wasn't ready to see her." Dr. Kurtsman started walking toward Kyle's room. "I am going to go check on him and see how he is feeling today. I can guess from the mad dash down the hall she just performed he has moved to the anger stage of grief. Why don't you come with me and we can here his side of the story."

Craig was still looking down the hall, watching the ghost of a crying young woman run away from yet more pain. He wanted to go after her but he trusted Dr. Kurtsman. After debating a few moments he turned and walked down the opposite direction to the elevator. He took it to the lobby and headed out to his car in the parking lot. He sent a quick text to Dr. Kurtsman telling him to say hello to Kyle for him but he had somewhere he needed to go. He promised to check in later and was still good to do dinner if everyone else was.

When he reached his car he slid behind the wheel but didn't start it right away. Instead he leaned back, closing his eyes. Several deep breaths later he was deciding what the best course of action would be and he realized how badly he wanted a drink. There was a bar just a couple of blocks over from the hospital and that made up his mind. He started the engine and put the car in drive.

The AA meeting he attended previously was at a church fifteen minutes away and there was one there today that started in twenty-five. He had plenty of time. He pulled into a space near the entrance and made his way in, grabbing a cup of coffee and a cookie. It was early but he thought the sugar might help clear his mind. He sat in the back just as he had before and as the meeting began he listened to the leader welcome everyone in. The man running the meeting asked if anyone would like to share. A number of hands went up and one by one they made their way forward to share triumphs and tribulations from the previous week. After several people spoke the man in charge asked if there was anyone else. Craig hesitantly raised his hand.

He was recognized and called forward. Just like the first time, he stood at the podium, taking in the gathered faces. He told them all that a girl named Rachel had been the catalyst for his coming and deciding it was time to get sober. His other group had lost her just over a week ago and they were still struggling to understand it all. And now they had lost another friend. A young man who needed help just as much, if not more, than the rest of them but refused to ask for or accept it.

He told them that several months ago he had lost his young son in a single car crash where he had been the driver and was diagnosed with PTSD as a result. It wasn't until the last couple of weeks he realized how much he needed to turn his life around and do better for those he loved. He lost his job, his wife, and his way but he is ready to start making the changes needed to live in a way that honors not only his son but also his recently lost friends.

When the meeting ended a man came up to him. He looked familiar but Craig wasn't sure why. "I was really sorry to hear about your friends. I'm a paramedic. I was there the night your friend Brian died, I am so sorry for your loss."

"Thanks." Craig looked at him. He recognized him as the man he had noticed watching him while he and Dr. Kurtsman sat on the porch steps.

"Is there anything I can do?" The man asked.

Craig shook his head with a sad smile. "I appreciate the offer but right now I am just trying to focus on recovery so I can find a new path in life where I can help others who really need it the way I have."

"Can I ask you something? I hope it isn't too personal." The medic looked nervous.

"I guess, yeah, go ahead."

"The single car crash you talked about, was that out on the edge of town in the Miller's field? If it brings up too many bad memories you have every right not to answer me." He instantly held up his hands in surrender, even though Craig hadn't reacted at all.

"It was actually. I guess situations like that are well known in a town this small." Craig said quietly. "I was in a fight with my wife. She was yelling at me and started shoving me. When I tried to calm her down I lost focus and control of the car. It ran off the road and wrapped around the big tree on the far side of the field. My son was killed in the crash and it has taken me a long time to stop blaming myself completely for the accident."

"Have you ever thought about becoming a paramedic? It is a great way to be there and help people when they really need it. There are hard times, like the night we got called out to your friend's house, and I was actually there the night of your accident." He swallowed hard. "I was one of the guys that cut the car apart to get your wife out of the car."

Craig stared at him in disbelief. "You were there?"

"Yeah, I knew the first time I saw you at a meeting last week I needed to talk to you but I was afraid of bringing it up. There are rough calls like those, but I swear there are more times when you get to help save a life or hold someone's hand as they recover and you get to be a part of their journey. It's something to think about. I can see what a big heart you have and it would be great if you thought about joining us."

Craig thought about everything he had just been told. It was a big shock. Here was someone who knew what he had been through and was in a similar situation fighting an addiction. If he could handle the desire to drink and still a job where he got to see the good and bad, maybe he could do it too. "I'll definitely think about it. I never thought about working in the medical field before but I love the idea of helping others heal. What's your name by the way?"

The man smiled and held out his hand to Craig. "I hope it works out for you. I'm Jeremy, nice to meet you."

# Chapter 22

While Craig was at his AA meeting, Dr. Kurtsman sat with Kyle. At first they said nothing. Dr. Kurtsman sipped from a bottle of water while Kyle stared at him, determined to stay quiet and wait out the doctor. Eventually he lost his patience. "Why are you here? What do you want from me?"

"I just came by to check in on you and see how you are feeling this morning." Dr Kurtsman shifted in his chair, trying to find a comfortable position.

Kyle's eyes narrowed and he folded his arms across his chest.
"The fact you even bother asking how I am feeling shows just how little you understand about what I am going through. How did you ever get to be in charge of a support group anyway? There is nothing you can do. Why don't you follow in that crybaby Jasmine's footsteps and leave?"

"I could always go home and work on my garden. My roses need some tending to." Dr. Kurtsman made no attempt to get up as he said this.

"Well go ahead then. There is no reason to be hanging around the hospital and nothing you can do for me." Kyle did his best to sound strong and defiant.

Dr. Kurtsman stood up, setting a bag on the seat and leaning on the back of the chair. He eyed Kyle, seeming to mull something over in his mind. "Did I ever tell you about my roses?"

Kyle stared at him. "No."

Dr. Kurtsman shrugged as though that made no difference. "My wife loved roses. My entire house is still decorated with them. It is floral from top to bottom in almost every room and in every corner of the garden there are rose bushes. One year I bought two new ones to plant as the centerpiece for a new garden she had created in the backyard. One of them was deep red, the other was white. I planted them together so they could grow together and intertwine, just like my wife and I."

Kyle listened. He had no idea where the story about roses could possibly be going. "Uh huh."

"The red bush put down roots and began to grow and flourish. It grew and blossomed but the white one wilted and began to slip away. I tried special plant food, watering schedules, anything I could think of, but it just continued to slowly die before my eyes. I lost the battle with the rose bush a year before my wife passed away. I hated the red roses after that. I cut off all of the flowers and moved the plants around it to other parts of the garden, forcing it to stand alone like I had to after she was gone."

Kyle tried to look uninterested, but despite himself, he wanted to know the rest of the story. He leaned forward. "What happened to the red bush?"

"It, too, began to wilt and die. I tried giving it fresh potting soil, that special food again, I even sat and talked to it when I was watering the plants. It took months of watching the rose bush struggle to realize what a delicate balance a garden is. The rose bush needed the other plants around it to keep it thriving. They were the support and the nourishment for the roses. I moved them back and did my best to tend to them all equally. The year after I put the garden back together I went out to work and saw my wife wasn't gone after all. She had left me a present in the roses." He stooped down and retrieved his bag. From inside he puled out a rose with a beautiful blossom in baby pink. He shuffled to the bed and handed it to Kyle.

The soldier hung his head and mumbled something under his breath while Dr. Kurtsman began to make his way out the door. He turned back for just a moment. "What was that?"

Kyle looked up with tears in his eyes. "Please tell Jasmine I'm sorry."

# Chapter 23

Dr. Kurtsman made his way into the hallway with a gentle smile on his face. Kyle and Jasmine would both recover from the confrontation that morning. They would also both move past their respective losses in time, he knew. They just needed to be willing to open up to supporting and being supported. Together, with Craig and Mandy, he believed they could all move forward if they were willing to do the work and step up when needed for one another.

He leaned heavily on his cane, almost doubled over from the effort of walking. He wheezed as he inched his way down the hall. He stared ahead at the bank of elevators but as he got close the edges of his vision began to darken and the world started spinning. He felt himself falling and managed to cry out for help before he lost consciousness and hit the ground.

Dr. Kurtsman woke up in the emergency room. The chemo he had been going through to attempt to slow the progression of his cancer had made him incredibly weak and he had contracted an infection which was now wreaking havoc inside him. The doctor standing over him was telling him all about what had happened and his mind said he needed to tell the group. He shook his head to clear the thought. They had enough to worry about at the moment, he wasn't going to burden them with his medical issues.

He closed his eyes, focusing on trying to breathe. He felt like he couldn't get enough air, like something was pressing on his chest. And the hope with the little nozzles shoving oxygen into his nose wasn't helping at all. He cracked one eye open and said nothing was preventing him from breathing. All of the people in the room continued to work around him but they all sounded like they were in another universe. HE closed the eye once more and tried again to focus on taking deep breaths. It seemed impossible but he knew he was just tired. It would get better like it always did.

He thought about Mandy. He hoped Jasmine would take her in the way she had with Rachel. Jasmine didn't know it and would deny it if anyone ever told her, but she had the makings of a great role model. Next he thought about Kyle. The loss of Brian would forever alter his life but he could see a strength in the young man and as long as he stayed open to healing and willing to share his struggles he had no doubt Kyle would do fine. Finally, Craig came to mind. He had noticed since Rachel's funeral the man no longer smelled of whisky and there had been a change in him at a deeper level as well. The pain of losing his son would never leave his heart but Dr. Kurtsman believed Craig would be able to move forward and channel that hurt into something positive as long as he stayed focused.

He felt the bed he was in as it began to move but he didn't bother opening his eyes. The doctors were just taking him for some test of another. What he needed at the moment was a nap to get his strength back up. He would see everyone at dinner that night and when he regained his energy he would talk to them and get them all on the right paths. Yes, as soon as he felt better he would get back to work.

# Chapter 24

Craig left the meeting feeling much better. He thought about his conversation with the paramedic, Jeremy, and the entire interaction felt like a sign from the universe. The man had the same name as his son. It was as though, somehow, his Jeremy was reaching out, telling him it was ok to move on and he approved of his father's desire to help people. It was true Craig never considered doing anything like working as an EMT before but he was looking for a drastic change and the opportunity to be there for someone going through a hard time could be exactly what he needed.

He was about to head home when the memory of Jasmine running from the hospital room crying floated up in his mind. She had been so upset. He knew Dr. Kurtsman had advised against talking to her but in his heart he couldn't get past the idea she needed someone to talk to, a friend. He drove around town, trying to think of anything he knew about her. He didn't want to call, he thought talking in person would be best. However, as he cruised the streets of Clydesburg he realized just how little he knew about her. She had kept everything so secret. He didn't know where she lived so he finally pulled out his phone and sent a quick text asking if she would be up for a chat. He got no response. He dialed the number but after several rings it went to voicemail. He wasn't sure if she was ignoring him or didn't have her phone with her. It was hard to imagine a girl her age being without her phone but in her emotional state she may have left it in her purse or car to have some quiet time.

He tried to think of the few things she told them. He ran through any favorite places and came up empty then focused on hobbies. That one he knew, she liked photography. He remembered she and Rachel spent time looking at pictures before and during the meetings. Rachel. She was the key. Suddenly, Craig knew where she must be.

He drove to the park. His first stop was the bench overlooking downtown but it was occupied by a couple, not Jasmine. He walked along the footpath, scanning both sides but there were very few people out at the moment. A few people with dogs and a trio of runners passed by but that was all. He was about to give up when he spotted the small pond at the far side of the park. A figure was sitting in the garden next to it and when he approached he could see it was Jasmine. She was sitting with her legs folded, staring at a white rose bush and crying.

His heart broke for her. He remembered at once that Rachel had died holding a white rose and he was almost positive Jasmine had given it to her. They probably got it while here at the park when they went to get the food and supplies.

"Jasmine?" He called softly. No reply. "Jasmine? Are you ok?"

She shifted but didn't look at him. She just stared at the roses. He sat next to her but not too close. He didn't know what to do at the moment. Part of him wanted to reach out and pat her hand or shoulder, anything to tell her he was there for her. The rest of him was convinced finding her had been wrong from the beginning.

"What do you want Craig?" Her eyes never left the roses.

"I came to check on you. I saw how upset you were this morning and just wanted to see if you were ok. I know this has been a terrible week for all of us and you were closer to Rachel than the rest of us."

"Why would you bother worrying about me? I'm nothing, not worth caring about." The flatness in her tone sent chills through him. She couldn't really believe that could she? He sat in silence, trying to figure out the best way to respond to that. It was so different from the strong persona she had displayed in the meetings. There he had seen a confident young woman, ready to heal and take on the world. Now, sitting in front of him, was a vulnerable girl who was scared and desperate to have anyone see her.

"You aren't nothing Jasmine. You are one of the most incredible young women I have ever known. You have the biggest heart and put everyone above yourself. Sometimes you need to hurt in order to heal. You have to let yourself be vulnerable and that is all this is. You have been there for everyone else and now it's your turn. I care about you. So did Rachel. Now Mandy has joined us. Kyle, and Dr. Kurtsman care about you. We are a family, just like Rachel thought we were."

Jasmine shook her head. "Kyle couldn't care less if I dropped dead. Hell, he would probably prefer it."

"You know that isn't true." Craig said.

"He said I was nothing." She looked over at him. "Those were his exact words."

"Look, I know you two had a fight. He is in pain. He lashed out over the frustration of losing his best friend. You know better than anyone how that feels. Remember your reaction to Mandy coming to the meeting this week?" He moved a little closer, keeping his voice low and the conversation just between them in case anyone else walked up. "You got so worked up you put yourself in the hospital with an anxiety attack."

Jasmine blushed at the memory and looked away. "Rachel was innocent. All she ever wanted was to live and be loved. I tried to be there for her and give her what she needed but I wasn't strong enough. I couldn't stop it, any of it."

She curled up on the grass and began crying again. Craig sat where he was , letting her mourn. He knew she thought she was hurting for Rachel but deep down he knew she was feeling all of the loss. Her tears fell for Rachel, for Brian, and for the pain in her own life she still couldn't face head on. She stayed there for several minutes until the sobs subsided. When she had herself under control again she sat back up and turned to face him. She asked him to tell her about his son.

He was completely taken aback by the request. He asked why she wanted to know and she told him it was the reason he came to the group. She wanted to know more about him. She realized too late she didn't know Rachel or Brian very well and if she had she may have seen the warning sighs and been able to be a better friend. Even though he didn't seem like he was on the verge of suicide she still wanted to be there for him and part of that was getting to know more about him.

Craig smiled and pulled up a picture on his phone. He said his son's name was Jeremy and he was a perfect little prince. He always obeyed his parents, was the perfect image of innocence and light, and loved to learn new things everyday. Jeremy was the reason he got up in the morning and there had been days he would watch his boy sleeping for a long time before he could make himself go to bed or even back to watch television with his wife. His son had been his breath of life and when he died it felt like he took a part of his heart and soul with him.

She took the phone and asked if she could look through other pictures of him. He nodded and she scrolled through, stopping on a picture of Craig holding him the day he was born. She looked up at him and smiled, saying she imagined he must look at them all the time.

He admitted he hadn't looked at any of them since the day Jeremy died. Her smiled melted away and a look of shock replaced it. She asked him why he wouldn't look at the pictures and he told her is was just too painful. She handed the phone back and looked over at the water and the roses again. "Is that why you drink? To forget about the pain?"

Now it was his turn to look up in surprise. "What makes you think I drink?"

She shrugged. "I have been able to smell it on you in the meetings. You always smelled like you had been at a bar before you came." His eyes dropped to the ground and she looked at him apologetically. "Sorry, I shouldn't have brought it up."

"No, it's fine. I guess I didn't realize it was so noticeable. I was drinking a lot and it started right after I got home from the hospital. But after we lost Rachel I sat in a bar, prepared to drink away that pain as well and realized I didn't want to honor her memory or my son's by forgetting about them. It hurts but I have been going to AA for a few meetings now. I'm trying to do better for them and for me."

Jasmine pulled her knees up to her chest and rested her arms on them, looking at him. "Did Dr. Kurtsman go home? I saw you guys in the hall when I went by earlier but I couldn't stay and chat."

Craig shrugged. "He went to talk to Kyle. After we saw you go running by I wanted to follow you and make sure you were ok then but he suggested we give you time to calm down. I went to a meeting and then decided you might need a friend after all. Why don't we give him a call and make sure dinner is still on."

She nodded and waited while he made the phone call. He sat quietly, listening to it ring but then frowned when a strange voice came on the line. He asked for Dr. Kurtsman and when the voice asked who was calling he identified himself and said he was part of the support group Dr. Kurtsman led. His face paled and he looked at Jasmine with wide eyes. He thanked the man on the phone and hung up, getting to his feet and holding out a hand to help her up. He told her Dr. Kurtsman had collapsed and was in the hospital himself now. His son had answered the phone and said things didn't look good. They needed to get back there right away.

# Chapter 25

Jasmine pulled into the parking lot of the hospital with Craig slamming his own car into park right behind her. She leapt from the car and took off running toward the front door. Craig was on her heels when he saw Kyle standing outside. He called for Jasmine to get inside and intercepted Kyle, quickly explaining what he knew and pulling him back inside.

They asked at the main information desk where he was located but were told the hospital can't give out information on patients to anyone outside of the family. Jasmine looked at Craig, tortured eyes begging him to come up with a solution. It took a moment but he did. He pulled his phone out and called Dr. Kurtsman's number again. Once more his son, James Jr. answered. When Craig explained the situation James told them he was with his father in the ICU. It was family only in the room but they could wait for him in the waiting area.

When they reached the ICU waiting room a few minutes later they found a man that looked exactly like Dr. Kurtsman, except thirty years younger, waiting for them. "I'm so glad you were able to make it."

"What happened?" Jasmine asked. "You told Craig on the phone he collapsed. Is he sick?"

James stared at her. "You all don't know?"

"Know what?" Craig and Kyle asked in unison.

"My father was a cancer survivor and had been in remission for years but it came back. This time it has been aggressive and he has been going through chemo just to slow the progression. It didn't really work and his body is shutting down now." James seemed to think deeply for a moment. Then, almost to himself, he continued.

"He was so focused on helping your little group get set up and begin the healing process he must have kept it from you so the knowledge wouldn't cause any further strain."

Craig looked around, wiping his hands on his jeans and dancing from foot to foot. Jasmine watched, thinking his fidgeting must be how he was dealing with the anxiety now that he wasn't drinking. His hands opened and closed as he searched the room for anything to do to feel useful. Eventually he looked between Jasmine and Kyle and then turned to James. "Is there a number for a Mandy in Dr. Kurtsman's phone?"

James opened the contacts and scrolled through. It took less than a minute to find the number and he handed the phone over to Craig who left the room to call and fill her in on what was happening. While Craig was gone James went back in to check on his father. Jasmine sat in one of the waiting room chairs and leaned her elbows on her knees with her face resting in her hands. She didn't cry. She didn't look like she had any tears left.

Kyle stood watching her for a long moment until she patted the chair next to her, the pain and frustration of their earlier fight forgotten. He sat next to her and, without thinking about it, placed an arm around her shoulders. Any other time she would have pulled away from a man trying to touch her but at that moment she just sat there. She whispered something to herself but before he could ask what it was she'd said, Craig came back in and told them Mandy was on her way. He had been surprised she wanted to come but there had been no hesitation in her voice. He took the chair next to Kyle and together, they waited.

Mandy arrived ten minutes later and walked right into the room, took the chair next to Jasmine and held her hand. Through exhausted, red-rimmed eyes Jasmine looked at the younger girl and smiled.

"Mandy, I am so sorry for the way I treated you. Please understand how much it hurt to lose Rachel who had become like a little sister to me even in just the short time I knew her, but that is no excuse for what happened and I am truly sorry. You are one of us, part of our family."

Mandy looked around at Craig and Kyle who smiled and nodded their agreement. She turned back to Jasmine and patted her hand but said nothing. Craig went in search of James to return the phone and thank him, as well as try for an update on Dr. Kurtsman. Kyle sat with the girls like a bodyguard, and let them cry together.

When Craig came back in and took his seat again Jasmine sat up and cleared her throat. "I am guessing we won't be going to dinner tonight."

"Is that what you whispered earlier?" Kyle asked her.

"No, I was thinking that too but I was just whispering a short prayer. I was asking Brian and Rachel to look over Dr. Kurtsman for us." She looked at him and saw the same pain in his eyes she felt in her heart.

"I think dinner might still be a good idea." Craig said, bringing the subject back. Everyone looked at him. "We are a family. We keep saying it. And if that includes all sitting together to enjoy a meal this evening I am up for it."

"It would mean a lot to me to join you all for dinner." Mandy added quickly.

"It sounds like it might be just what the doctor ordered." Kyle said with an attempt at a grin.

Jasmine stared at the faces around her, studying them each for a long time before she finally nodded her agreement. James came back out to say Dr. Kurtsman was resting comfortably at the moment. Craig informed him they were going to be going to dinner later but he would appreciate any updates James was willing to provide. He made sure he left his number then went home to work on a few chore around the house and said he would meet everyone later.

The girls decided to go to the PJ Cafe to get coffee and some snacks and talk a little more. They asked Kyle if he would like to join them after James had gone back into the ICU again but he delcined. He said he thought he would stick around in case James needed to talk or there was any way he could help. Jasmine held out her hand and when he took it to shake, she pulled him up into an embrace. "We're going to get through this, all of it." She whispered in his ear. "We're family and we support each other, that's what families do."

# Chapter 26

Kyle sat in the waiting area staring at his phone. There seemed to be a million people he should call but none felt like the right first call to make. He thought about the funeral arrangements that would need to be made and wondered if he was the right person to be doing it. That was enough to decide the call order.

He dialed Dylan's number. He was sure the police had made a notification by then but he hadn't heard anything from Brian's younger brother. He listened as it rang then clicked over to voicemail. He left a message saying who it was and that they needed to talk so please call when he got a chance. When he disconnected from Dylan he called Rafael Riveria, now truly the only other survivor beside himself from Afghanistan and the firefight that seemed to sum up their deployment.

They chatted for a few minutes about how things were going after returning from Arlington, future plans, and families. When he couldn't put it off any longer Kyle told Riveria that Brian was gone. He didn't go into detail but explained the highlights of what happened. Riveria said he was sorry to hear about Nickerson and asked how Kyle was holding up. He offered to come back out and visit again, even to stay through whatever memorial service was planned. Kyle didn't have the heart to tell him at the moment nothing was in the works but he knew they would get it sorted out soon. Instead he told Riveria he would love to see a friendly face and to text him the travel information once he had it.

As he was hanging up with Rafael, Dylan called back. He told Kyle he had been out camping for the last few days and when he got home there was a message from the Clydesburg Police to call. He did and they informed him Brian had died. He asked Kyle to confirm what he was told which he did. Dylan was so quiet after that he wondered briefly if Dylan had hung up. Finally he spoke again and said his brother had always been troubled. He hoped the Army would have helped but he was just a younger version of their father and that wasn't all good. He asked how Kyle was doing and said he would start packing to head home as soon as they were off the phone. He was an English professor in Michigan but could find someone to cover his classes for a week or so.

Dylan asked Kyle if he wanted to make the funeral arrangements or wait until he got there. Kyle told him he honestly didn't know which way would be best and suggested they discuss it when he arrived. He told Dylan about Riveria coming and said he had a few ideas of a couple other military guys that might want to come but other than that he wasn't sure who to tell. Dylan told him not to stress about it for now. They would sit down and talk about it more when he got home. He was going to be looking for flights and would call with his landing information as soon as he could.

Kyle hung up and stared at the floor. He put the phone back in his pocket and rubbed his face, feeling the two day old stubble on his cheeks. He knew he must look awful. Just then he noticed a young boy sitting on the floor nearby, staring at him. The boy was playing with a toy truck while his parents sat behind him and talked in hushed tones. He did his best to smile at the boy who raced his truck across the carpet in front of him. When he got to Kyle's feet, the boy looked up and asked what was wrong. Kyle looked down the hall toward Dr. Kurtsman's room and said he was just worried about a friend. The boy said his grammpa is sick. He said his mom said grammpa is sleeping right now but he hopes he wakes up soon because he wants to race his truck and grammpa has the other one.

Kyle looked up to see the parents talking to a nurse. The mother was crying and gesturing toward the rooms. He got the feeling "grammpa" was done racing trucks. He looked back down and asked the boy what his name was. The boy smiled showing off his missing front teeth. "My name is Brian, Brian Delune. What's yours?"

"My name is Kyle Masters." He told him, trying to disguise the pain of hearing Brian's name. "My best friend in the whole wide world is named Brian too."

"Did you ever race trucks?" Little Brian asked him.

"We sure did." Kyle told him, moving to sit on the floor with the boy.

"Do you have your truck with you? If you do we could all race when grammpa and your friend wake up." Kyle smiled at the boy's single tracked focus. He remembered being that age with nothing more complicated than climbing a tree or playing basketball all day on his mind.

"Sorry buddy, I don't have mine with me. Can I see your truck though?" The boy's hand had been covering the majority of the truck while he rolled it around, leaving only the wheels showing. Now he took his hand off and Kyle could see it was an ARMY Hummer. The boy beamed with excitement as Kyle looked at it. He said someday he is going to drive a real one and be a hero like the soldiers he saw on television. A hero like grammpa and make him proud because they are best friends.

Kyle was overcome with emotion as he handed the truck back. Brian continued without noticing the change in Kyle. He said grammpa gave him the truck for Christmas before he got sick. He looked over his truck, spinning one of the wheels. "Grammpa said best friends are always there, even when you can't see them. When they are at their own houses or on vacation, even when they go to sleep forever and watch over us from the sky, even then they are still our best friends. Then they keep us safe until we can all be together and play trucks again. Grammpa said it isn't our fault when they go to sleep forever and into the sky. Sometimes God just needs them more than we do. Grammpa is really smart."

"You're right, grammpa is very smart and I bet he would be so happy to know how much you like the truck he gave you." Brian smiled at him.

"Brian? Come here sweetie." Kyle looked up to see Brian's mother gesturing for her son to come back over to her as she wiped tears from her eyes.

"That's my mom." He told Kyle matter-of-factly. "We come visit grammpa everyday. Will you be here tomorrow?"

"I'm not sure yet, maybe." Kyle got up and slid back into the chair.

"If you do come, maybe you can bring your truck and we can race together." Brian's eyes lit up at the prospect. Kyle agreed if he came tomorrow he would bring his fastest truck and they could race. One look over Brain's shoulder at the weeping mother told Kyle Brian wouldn't be back tomorrow or any day in the near future. He told Brian to take care as he ran back to his parents. Kyle watched them exit the waiting room. He wanted to hug little Brian and shield him from finding out his best friend had died. At the same time he smiled as the words echoed in his heart, best friends are always with you.

His best friend had sent him a sign through a little boy with the same name. His brother was still watching over him. When he sat down with Dylan and Riveria he would make sure they remembered him for the man he truly was, not just the rough edges. He was a soldier and a badass, but he was also someone who adopted a lost and lonely foster kid and gave him a family and a home. With his arms folded and his head bowed as if in prayer, Kyle finally began to cry.

He cried for the brothers lost in combat and the survivors struggling like himself. It wasn't about who made it home to walk the streets of their home towns and who made the ultimate sacrifice, the scars were there on all of them. He cried for Rachel and the innocence lost during her attack. Tears ran down for Craig and the pain he carried after losing his son. His heart broke for Dr. Kurtsman who never stopped missing his late wife. He wept for the Brian's big and small who felt the pain of real life far too deeply. He felt for Jasmine as she struggled to heal from scars both visible and hidden. But mostly, he took time to cry for himself and the strength he tried to show even what he really wanted was a hug and to let others be there for him and show him he wasn't alone.

The group was a family. They said it and they meant it. He had done his best to be there for the others and he was ready to admit he needed someone to be there for him at the moment. When Dr. Kurtsman got better he would be happy to see the growth the group had experienced through his lead.

# Chapter 27

Mandy went with Jasmine back to her parent's house after they left the coffee shop. They talked excitedly about summer plans and ideas for a memorial for Rachel and Brian. Mandy said she wasn't sure how many kids from school would want to come but since Rachel had died many of them seemed to realize how awful they had been to her and felt bad she was pushed so far.

When they walked in Georgia was holding a letter up to the light, trying to see what was inside of it. "Mom, what are you doing?"

Georgia jumped, dropping the envelope. "You got a letter from some mentoring company. I was just trying to see what it was about, that's all."

Jasmine's face burned and she looked at the ground. "Rachel suggested I apply for a program over the summer where I could take a master class from world renowned photographers. I didn't tell her I took her advice, I wanted to see if I would get in first."

"Really?" Mandy asked, her eyes shining. "I applied to the same program. I got in. I just found out yesterday. If you're in too we can hang out all summer, if you want to of course."

Jasmine gave her a side hug then bent down to retrieve the letter from the floor. She opened the envelope cautiously, as though it might bite her. Once it was open the word at the top of the page was visible and both girls squealed together. Staring back at her was the word Congratulations!

Mandy grinned and suggested maybe part of the memorial they put together could include some of the pictures taken during the meeting where the made the posters. Jasmine nodded but he smile had already begun to fade. "What if I'm not good enough? What if everyone hates me? What if I just embarrass their memories?"

Georgia wrapped her daughter in her arms." Nothing like that is going to happen. Besides, what your doing is coming from the heart so there is no way it can be embarrassing or wrong."

Jasmine hugged her mom back then held open an arm to bring Mandy into the fold. She suggested they share their good news when they met up with Kyle and Craig for dinner then they could all go up to the hospital and see how Dr. Kurtsman was doing afterward. Mandy nodded, still enjoying the group hug. Jasmine's heart soared. Things were finally looking up.

# Chapter 28

Riveria and Dylan both landed before the group was scheduled to meet for dinner. Kyle picked them both up and drove to the restaurant to have a drink before the others arrived. They discussed Brian's funeral and agreed to keep it extremely small. They would only invite the rest of the support group and the three of them. He was a showman and believed he was larger than life but he would never want to be remembered for the way he died.

Kyle told the two men about the support group and how much it felt like it had helped him. He told them about losing Rachel and how he wished more people had the ability to talk to people before it was too late. Riveria admitted he had been working with a therapist to deal with lingering trauma over what they saw while they were deployed. Dylan shared some memories of his brother and they all toasted to their fallen friend and brother.

When Craig, Mandy, and Jasmine arrived Kyle made introductions and they all sat down. Before anyone could even look at the menu Mandy blurted out the news that she and Jasmine got into a summer photography program and would like to use the knowledge they would gain to create a memorial for Brian and Rachel. She said they would be the final projects for the program and would be displayed at a local gallery when the class was finished. Kyle said he thought it sounded like a perfect idea and both Dylan and Riveria said they would do their best to make it back to see it when they were done.

Craig seemed distracted throughout dinner, only making one and two word comments now and then. When they were getting up to leave his phone vibrated in his pocket. He pulled it out and frowned at the unfamiliar number. He answered it and dropped heavily back into his chair. The caller was James, Dr. Kurtsman had just passed away.

# Epilogue

They all sat back down. James had said he would come over and talk to them at the restaurant. The conversation had all but stopped and when James arrived the table was practically silent. He said he didn't have a lot of time but he wanted to explain things in person. The cancer had weakened Dr. Kurtsman's body to such an extent when he collapsed his body started to shut down. He only regained consciousness a few times and in those periods he had made his final wishes known.

He had life insurance that would cover his expenses and leave an inheritance for his son. However, in the last week or so, he had set money aside and wanted it to be given to the members of the support group to help them follow their dreams and continue healing. They all looked around, stunned. James told them he was exhausted but he had wanted to give them news directly. He said he would be in touch to get them the money his father wanted them to have then gave each member a hug or handshake. Just before he left he looked at them and said he wanted to thank them for making his father's life so happy the last few months. With that, he left. The group looked at one another but words failed them all. They hugged one another and agreed to keep in touch, then all made their way to their respective homes.

Dr. Kurtsman's funeral was held three days later. The service was well attended and the wake after showed the members of the group just how loved their leader had been. James Jr. introduced a few friends and family members to them and they shared their experiences with Dr. Kurtsman. At the end of the memorial Kyle quietly let them know there was also going to be a service for Brian the next day. His was much smaller.

Dylan, Riveria, Kyle, Mandy, Jasmine and her mom Georgia, Craig and his sister Caroline, and James Kurtsman Jr. all gathered to pay their respects. Even with the tiny group Kyle wanted to speak on behalf of his friend and at the cemetery there was a twenty gun salute and Taps was played. Brian was buried next to his father and the group shared tears and hugs as they said goodbye.

The group split up after that. Kyle returned to duty and switched into recruiting so he could stay close to home. Riveria deployed with his infantry division but stayed in touch with Kyle through emails and social media. Dylan returned to Michigan and his teaching job while Craig disappeared with no communication with anyone. Jasmine and Mandy completed their photography program and sent out invitations for everyone to join them at their end of summer showcase.

Everyone except Riveria, who was serving somewhere in the Middle East, came to see their work and congratulated them on a job well done. They noted Dr. Kurtsman, Brian, and Rachel were all well represented and honored through their pictures.

They all shared what they have been up to and when it got to be his turn Craig told them he was training to be a first responder paramedic so he can help people like the men and women who saved his life and worked so hard to save his son. He apologized for being drunk around them when they first met and said he is sober now. He also told them, with the help of his lawyer sister, he got permission to do something he would like to share with them. The all accompanied him to the park Jasmine and Rachel used to visit and followed him down to the pond. He created a small memorial garden within the larger one in the names of those they lost.

He told them he learned butterflies were a symbol of healing because partway through life they hide away but then are reborn into something new and beautiful. He then showed them a tattoo of a butterfly with the names of their three heavenly members around it. The last thing he wanted to show them was a collection of butterflies he got and said it would mean the world to him if they would all help him release the butterflies in honor of their journeys and the new chapters they are all starting in their healing as well as the angels who got their wings and are now watching over them.

   With tears in their eyes but smiles on their faces, they all held butterflies in cupped hands. They whispered prayers and loving words then let them go, watching as they rose toward the sky. Their new lives were beginning and their friends would always be in their hearts. Now it was time to spread their own wings and learn to fly.

Made in the USA
Middletown, DE
24 September 2023